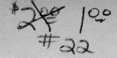

"What's going on here, Sergeant?"

"Why nothing at all, Corporal. We're just gonna stretch us some bushwhacker necks."

George Thayre began to cry, the tears rolling down his face as he pleaded, "My god, men, don't do this. We've all got wives and children back home. We're innocent . . ."

"Listen to this sniveling whelp," Birch taunted. "Can't even die like a man."

Corporal Abbott walked to where Alexander stood leaning against a tree and saluted. "Sir, you can't let them do this. It's monstrous. We're southerners, sir. No true southerner would ever take part in this . . ."

Alexander looked away and said coldly, "Then don't take part in it."

Bill Sawyer had managed to struggle to his feet in spite of his hands being tied behind his back and now he stared at Smackler and said, "For God's sake, Sergeant, if you have to do this, then shoot us. We don't deserve hanging like some common murderers . . ."

LEATHERHAND

#5 BAD DAY AT BANDERA

MIKE WALES

PINNACLE BOOKS NEW YORK

LEATHERHAND #5: BAD DAY AT BANDERA

Copyright © 1984 by Mike Wales

An original Pinnacle Books edition, published for the first time anywhere.

First printing / October 1984

ISBN: 0-523-42191-5

Can. ISBN: 0-523-43181-3

Cover art by Bruce Minney

Printed in the United States of America

PINNACLE BOOKS, INC.
1430 Broadway
New York, New York 10018

9 8 7 6 5 4 3 2 1

BAD DAY AT BANDERA

Chapter 1

The old gunfighter known as the Preacher sat with his back solidly planted against a boulder and watched the flames of his small campfire leap and cavort with the night's soft breezes as they ate away at the snarled mesquite limbs.

It was cold on the banks of the Nueces River in southwest Texas, even though spring was just around the corner. As the Preacher leaned forward to toss more fuel on the fire, the flames played over the saturnine plains of a face that had weathered seventy-three years in some of the toughest and wildest country in America. Perhaps it was those years of living out of his saddlebag that had made him more aware of the cold now. Lifting his head, he peered into the darkness from eyes that were as clear as the day he turned twenty-one.

Nothing stirred and the Preacher's big black stud continued to graze complacently. The horse was a better guard dog than any hound, and the old gunfighter knew it would react immediately to prowlers of the night.

Pulling his heavy blanket over his legs, he reached his right hand for the coffeepot simmering on the edge of the fire, lifted it carefully and poured a tin cup half full, returned the pot and sipped at the brew.

Then the horse raised its head and looked to the east. The Preacher drank deeply, set the cup down and rose and casually checked his wood supply, then walked easily into the darkness, vanishing as suddenly as if whisked away by some evil spirit. Fifty feet from his fire he took up a position beside a large boulder, making sure it covered his back, and, with hands swinging freely above the twin butts of a pair of heavy Colt .45s, waited.

He didn't have long in the night's chilly breezes. A rider suddenly materialized from near where the Preacher's stud was staked out and the beautiful Appaloosa he rode nickered softly and was answered just as softly by the black.

The Appy's rider was a tall young man who could have been anywhere from twenty-five to thirty years old. He was dressed casually in a working cowboy's garb, including a heavy pair of bullhide chaps. On his head a flat-crowned gambler's gray hat sat back from his high forehead and on his hip he wore a single pistol, a heavy .44 in an open holster. The hand that never strayed far from the gun was covered by a peculiar leather contraption that resembled a glove, yet was not.

Stopping twenty feet from the fire, the man dismounted, uncinched his saddle and, while the Appy stood ground-tied, carried it to the fire and dropped it, then went and removed the bridle and watched the big horse move off and immediately drop and roll in the loose soil. Digging into his saddlebags, the man brought out a curry comb and brush and, when the horse regained its feet, carefully cleaned away the dirt and sweat marks and then left it to feed unrestrained. It immediately went to the stud, touched noses with the big black and snorted.

Returning to the fire, the tall man bent and dug out a coffee cup from his small pack and helped himself to the pot, then hunkered down, apparently unconcerned that he had invaded another man's camp.

Five minutes later, the Preacher came out of the darkness and dropped a load of wood near the fire, nodded wordlessly at his visitor and went away again, returning after a few minutes with more wood.

Dropping it he stood, bent backward with his hands on his hips, and observed, "Me, I reckon I'm getting too damned old for this kinda game."

His visitor grinned. "You'll be old when they hit you in the face with a shovel."

Sitting back down against his rock, the Preacher asked. "Well, Vent Torrey, what brings you gallivanting all over south Texas?"

"Looking for you," Vent said.

"Heard they plugged you up in northern California . . ."

"Wrong information," Vent assured him. "Got a little piece of me here and there, but I'm still riding the same saddle."

"You seen Cam Spencer or Owney Sharp?"

"Owney's dealing faro at Tom Anderson's place at Silver City, New Mexico, and Cam, he decided to hang around northern California. He's the city badge in Yreka."

The Preacher filled his coffee cup and drank the hot fluid as if it were spring water. "See you still got the Appy . . ."

"Yep. Me and that old horse, we go back a long way," Vent said, and the Preacher looked at his visitor's leather-covered hand and said softly, "Leatherhand. They talk about you all the way down into Mexico and even back East."

"Some shuckins', now ain't I?" Vent said sourly.

"With a rep like that you better be," the old man said, and pulled the blanket over his legs. "This here cold seems to dig right in and work at my bones."

Vent's grin changed his whole face. Suddenly he was no longer the hard-faced man with a gun, but a youth filled with lighthearted thoughts and a certain devilment that only a very few men had ever seen.

The Preacher would have sighed if that had been his nature. He liked this deadly young man whose gun reputation was one of the most fearsome in the West, but he liked him even more when he was like this: a man with no cares and no enemies.

Then Vent's smile faded and the enemies were once again peopling the night shadows and the ghosts of the twenty-nine men he had put down peered over his shoulder and cackled in silent laughter as they did all his waking hours, sometimes even coming to haunt him in his sleep.

The Preacher knew about this. He too had buried his share of men, and sometimes they came back to stand and look at him with awful accusing eyes and outstretched hands that begged for another chance. He knew he would carry them to the grave and probably meet them beyond even life itself.

"How's the hand these days?" he asked, looking at Vent's leather-covered right hand.

Holding it up, Vent said, "As good as it always was. When that Ute shaman out there in Colorado fixed me up with this contraption, he knew what he was about."

The preacher, like most everybody in the West at that time, knew the story behind the leather-covered hand. Vent Torrey had come to Colorado from Kansas, where he was the lone male survivor of a family that had feuded with another family named Hawks down in Missouri for more years than the last of the clan could recall. It was said that each side built its own cemetery, and the dead numbered more than five hundred before Vent fired the final shot at a lonely railroad station in the mountains of Colorado.

He would not have fired that shot if it hadn't been for an Indian named Swift Wind, whose son Vent had saved from drowning. The Indian, noting Vent's crippled gunhand, shot through by a Hawkses' bullet, made a leather glove with straps that reinforced it to the point where it was as good or better than ever. Months of practice under the tutelage of a gunfighting gambler turned Vent into a wizard with the .44 his father had given him when he was nine years old.

"How many times have you had new gloves made?" the Preacher asked curiously.

"This is the seventh," Vent said, and tossed more wood on the fire.

The Preacher shook his head. "That Injun sure enough knew what he was about. He'd of made one hell of a doctor."

"He is a hell of a doctor; one of the Ute tribe's top shamans," Vent assured him.

They fell silent, each with his secret thoughts, and the minutes crawled by. Then the Preacher cleared his throat and asked, "You lookin' for me for any particular reason?"

Vent, who had been remembering a widow at Yreka who had asked him to stay on and help her run her ranch, looked up and grinned. "Why hell, I ran into Arkie Chan at Dogville and he said he crossed your trail at Black Hawk. Said you was on a gun job for a relative and could use some help. Thought I'd drift along and offer my gun if it ain't shooting the governor of Texas or some such."

"I was dealing poker at the Tollgate Saloon when Arkie came in," the Preacher said. "I reckon I did mention it. Thought maybe he might want to join in the festivities, but he promised Tom Anderson he'd come up and help him out."

"I'm here," Vent said simply, and waited, knowing the

Preacher would get around to explaining in his own good time.

"I got me a nephew. Nice young feller comes from up in Williamson County. He's got him a vow to keep and I reckon I'm gonna help him keep it."

They had left Williamson County, eight men and a boy who had just turned sixteen two days after the Fourth of July, and were on their way to Mexico. Bill Sawyer was their leader and it had been he who had convinced the others they had no part in this crazy war between the states. Texas had seceded from the Union, but that didn't mean they had to go off and fight for it.

"We're going to Mexico," Sawyer had said. "We can just sit down there and wait her out. Hell, this fight, she ain't gonna go on forever. When it's all over, we come back home."

It sounded like a good idea and the others—Bill Sawyer's brother, the tall one they called CJ; and George Thayre; Bill Shumahe, who was always chewing tobacco; Jack Whitmire, the half-pint among them; Jake Kyle with the big mouth; John Smart, the husky young man who wanted to be a preacher and seldom spoke; and Old Man Vanwinkle with the white beard and no first name—went along with Bill Sawyer. They didn't want to fight either. They didn't figure the war was any of their doings anyhow.

Jimmie Watson, whose father and mother had died when their west Texas house burned to the ground with them trapped inside, worked for Sawyer, so he just naturally went along too.

They passed through Bandera in southeast Texas on their way to the Mexican border on July 21, 1863, and stopped just long enough to purchase supplies and some extra equipment and ammunition. The guns they carried were not for defense or offense against either the North or

South, but protection against the fierce border Indian tribes who savagely attacked and murdered small bands of travelers, taking advantage of the lack of troops, most of which had been sent off to fight in the war.

However, twelve miles north of Bandera, Camp Verde was home to a troop of Confederate cavalry. It was a hard post and the men were bored with army life, complaining bitterly that they had signed up to fight damn Yankees and not to hibernate out in Texas three states away from the actual fighting.

Major W. J. Alexander, a product of the southern aristocracy and a man who hated his present assignment, believing he had been deliberately sidelined from the war because of politics, was second in command at the camp. He was as bored as his men.

It was late afternoon when a rider came into the sutler's store and bought a sack of tobacco and some rifle shells and mentioned casually to the hard-bitten sergeant behind the counter, "Just came up from Bandera. Feller down there told me a bunch of bushwhackers passed that way a day or two ago. Bought some supplies and a whole passel of rifle and pistol balls."

"The hell you say?" the sergeant said, and shook his head. "Reckon somebody oughta tell the colonel about this. Reckon he might want to know who's riding around his territory."

"Go ahead and tell him," the man said, and walked out, mounted the U-necked excuse for a horse he had come in with, and left the camp at a lumbering gallop. Watching him go, the sutler suddenly turned his head and shouted, "You, Billy D! Come watch the store. I gotta go see the colonel," and not waiting for the private to come from the back platform where he had been sitting playing mumbly peg with a huge Barlow knife, the sergeant hurried across the compound and entered the commander's outer office.

"Gotta see the colonel," he told the fuzz-faced corporal sitting at the desk, and, not waiting for proper clearance, went and knocked on the commander's door, then entered, saluted and stood at attention.

Major Alexander sat slouched back in a hard chair near the window peering out into the compound, his eyes greedily devouring the slim body of Sergeant Smackler's wife, who was hanging out her washing.

Colonel Charles Underhill, commanding the camp and its crew of misfits, was a man who loved food. His bulging belly gave ample proof of that. As he glanced up at Sergeant Grady and cleared his throat, Alexander, who never tired of watching the rotund colonel play at being a soldier, waited to see what this new development would offer in the way of entertainment.

"What is it, Grady?" the colonel asked tiredly, as if the entire weight of the Confederate Army rested on his shoulders alone.

"Sir, a feller just stopped at the store. Said a whole company of bushwhackers rode through Bandera a couple of days ago. He said they bought enough rifle and pistol ammo to hold off half the Confederate Army."

The colonel cleared his throat and, glancing at the major, whose face remained blandly indifferent, said, "Probably long gone by now."

"Feller said they rode south," the sergeant said.

Alexander, bored stiff, suddenly rose and said crisply, "Sir, don't you think it might be a good idea for me to take a company and ride down there and investigate? If it is a bunch of Union sympathizers, they could cause a lot of problems this far west."

The colonel nodded, his jowly cheeks bouncing up

and down as he said, "Good idea, major. Take twenty-five men and draw rations for six days. Check it out."

Saluting smartly, Alexander turned, said shortly, "Let's go, Grady," and marched from the colonel's office.

As the door closed, Underhill snorted, growled, "Popinjay," and began watching Smackler's wife. Then he went to the door and said, "Corporal, you go tell Alexander to take Sergeant Smackler with him. He's the best scout we got."

The corporal duly passed on the order and the major looked toward the colonel's office, then to where Smackler's wife was bending over her washtub, and thought, I hope she kicks him right where it hurts, and began rounding up his men.

Two days later, he rode into the adobe store and livery stable in Hondo and asked the proprietor if he had noticed men riding through.

"Why, yes sir, Major. Eight or nine fellers came through here. They was real polite. Paid for what they bought and said they was on their way to Mexico. Said they was going where they didn't have to fight in no war."

Smackler, a powerfully built man from the hills of Tennessee, where he'd met his wife, spat a thin line of tobacco juice into the dry dust of the street and said to Corporal Duane Abbott, "Like hell they was peaceable. More like they was planning on a raid somewheres."

Abbott, whose father was a preacher, had been taught to give the other fellow the benefit of the doubt. "Maybe, but we sure as hell should check them out first. Might be innocent fellers just going into Mexico to buy cattle or something."

Smackler snorted. "What we ought to do is hang the bastards."

Abbott did not answer. Smackler scared hell out of him. They moved on and reached Squirrel Creek in late afternoon. As they passed through a stand of oak, one of the men rode back from the flank and said, "Major, they's a campfire up ahead."

Alexander held up his hand and brought the company to a halt, then signaled Sergeant Smackler and Sergeant Baldy Birch up front. "You boys take half the company each and circle their camp. I'll walk in and order them to surrender. If they resist, cut 'em down."

Bill Sawyer was just bending over to refill his plate when the major suddenly stepped from the bushes and called out in a loud voice, "Stand still. We've got you surrounded. You're under arrest. Resist and you die. Come along peaceable and you'll get a fair trial at Camp Verde."

The eight men and the boy sitting around the fire sprang to their feet and hastily raised their hands.

As the brush suddenly erupted soldiers in gray, Sawyer stared in bewilderment, then asked nobody in particular, "What the devil's goin' on? We ain't done nothing."

Alexander walked up to them and said, "You bushwhackers are under arrest. You gonna give up your weapons?"

Sawyer stepped forward and said politely, "Why certainly, Major. But, we're not bushwhackers. We're peaceable men going about our own affairs. We've got nothing to hide. We'll be happy to stand trial."

Smackler swaggered among the travelers and gathered up their rifles and handguns and piled them near a packhorse a trooper had led into the clearing.

CJ Sawyer stepped up beside his brother and asked, "What's this all about, Major?"

"Who are you?" the major challenged.

"Why, I'm CJ Sawyer and this here's my brother, Bill. We all come from Williamson County," he said, staring around uneasily at the hard-faced troopers who now surrounded them in a solid wall of gray.

Turning to Sergeant Birch, Alexander snapped, "Get

these here bushwhackers' names and tie their hands behind them. Put them on their horses and let's get away from here. Could be they are on their way to meet a bigger force. This could be a trap."

Looking at Alexander's sullen mouth and bitter eyes, Bill Sawyer was frightened. He did not like the ugly looks that were being passed back and forth between the troopers. He knew full well the penalty meted out to bushwhackers, those hit-and-run border fighters who rode out in civilian dress and struck at ranches in isolated areas, laying waste to them and murdering their owners. Hanging was the accepted punishment and there were no exceptions.

Looking at his brother with a sinking heart, he was filled with a terrible foreboding that he would never see his wife and children again.

Jack Kyle strutted up to the major and said, "Major, we've done nothing. You have no right to arrest us. We're honest men minding our own business."

"Get back with the others," Alexander snapped.

"Now see here, Major, my father's a prominent man in Texas," Kyle persisted. "He ain't gonna take kindly to you fellers arresting me."

Looking at Smackler, Alexander asked, "You get this man's name?"

Smackler nodded. "Yes sir. It's Jake Kyle. Says he's from east Texas."

Abbott, who was raised around San Antonio, stepped up and said, "Sir, I've heard of the Kyle family. They own a big spread in east Texas. Raise some fine horses, they do."

Alexander did not like Corporal Abbott. He did not believe a man who wanted to be a preacher could also become a good fighting man. "Corporal," he said, "did it ever occur to you that this man might have borrowed that name? For that matter, every last one of these bushwhackers could have taken on somebody else's name as a cover."

Abbott, a stubborn young man, shook his head. "Sir, I've seen several Kyles. They all look alike. This gent resembles the family."

Tired of arguing, Alexander snapped, "Get back to your duties, Corporal. Let me make the decisions around here. That's why I'm wearing the boards and you are wearing stripes."

Several of the troopers had heard the exchange and now they looked at their prisoners with some doubt.

Alexander, his back as stiff as a ramrod, led his company north, and two days later they camped near the Bandera hills. All that day Smackler and Birch had been moving from one man to the next, arguing that once the bushwhackers were returned to the fort, they would get off scot-free.

"We don't want that, now do we?" Smackler asked Private Timkins, a slim nineteen-year-old bugler from New Orleans. The boy shook his head.

Now the prisoners sat in a row fifty feet from the campfire where a cook was preparing a meal. Four troopers with ready rifles stood guard. Suddenly, Smackler rose and spoke to the major. "Sir, we've decided to hang these here bushwhackers. We figure if we take them back to camp, they'll get off. Hell, sir, you know how the colonel is. He'd let 'em go for certain sure."

Alexander stared at him. "Without a trial, Sergeant?" He raised an eyebrow inquiringly; his lips twisted sardonically.

Looking down at him where the major lay sprawled on a blanket, Smackler wondered if the man had been drinking. He had long suspected the officer was a secret drinker but had never caught him with a bottle to his mouth. "We don't need no trial for a bunch of dirty bushwhackers," he snarled.

Birch came up then and said, "Sir, I agree with Sergeant Smackler. I say we hang them."

Alexander stood up and, placing his hands on his hips, asked, "You declaring this army a democracy, Sergeant?"

"No sir, just trying to convince you of the right of it," Birch said lamely.

"You think hanging eight men and a sixteen-year-old boy's the right thing to do?" Alexander asked.

"We didn't figure to stretch the kid's neck," Smackler said.

"What you gonna do with him?" Birch wanted to know.

"We'll take him back to the camp. Send him along to Fredericksburg. They'll take care of him there."

Alexander smiled. "Nice. Send a boy off to that hellhole. He'll never survive it."

"That's his tough luck," Smackler said. "Hell, we didn't ask him to join this here bunch anyway, Major."

Alexander turned and walked off, saying, "Do as you damn please, Sergeant. It makes little difference to me."

Smackler marched over to the prisoners. "You prisoners stand up."

As they struggled to their feet, several troopers stood watching them.

"What's going on?" Old Man Vanwinkle asked. "When do we get fed?"

"Where you're going, old man, you won't need food," a sour-faced trooper named Pete Jolly taunted him.

Corporal Dan Malone strode over and said harshly, "Let's get this here job done. You men walk over here," and he led them to where a huge oak tree stood. Gazing up into its branches, Malone said, "This will do just fine. Andy, fetch the ropes."

Sawyer's face filled with alarm. "Wait. You agreed to deliver us to Camp Verde. You can't do this."

"The hell we can't, you dirty bushwhacker," Birch snarled,

and knocked Sawyer down. When his brother would have gone to his aid, one of the troopers jerked him back into line.

Abbott came hurrying over and stared at the men and the oak tree. "What's going on here, Sergeant?"

"Why nothing at all, Corporal. We're just gonna stretch us some bushwhacker necks."

George Thayre began to cry, the tears rolling down his face he pleaded, "My god, men, don't do this. We've all got wives and children back home. We're innocent . . ."

"Listen to this sniveling whelp," Birch taunted. "Can't even die like a man."

Abbott walked to where Alexander stood leaning against a tree and saluted. "Sir, you can't let them do this. It's monstrous. We're southerners, sir. No true southerner would ever take part in this . . ."

Alexander looked away and said coldly, "Then don't take part in it," and walked to where the troops were gathered watching the frightened prisoners. "You men, any of you who don't want to take part in this has my permission to stand down."

More than half of the twenty five moved off a little way and stood staring at the condemned men. Glancing around, Smackler noted that Ted Hunnacker, Anselamo Contreas, Buel Courtney and Ed Canto still faced the prisoners.

Bill Sawyer had managed to struggle to his feet in spite of his hands being tied behind his back and now he stared at Smackler and said, "For God's sake, Sergeant, if you have to do this, then shoot us. We don't deserve hanging like some common murderer. . . ."

"Suit yourself." Birch drew and fired from the hip. His bullet tore into Sawyer's right side, knocking him off his feet and into a bundle of writhing agony.

Turning his head, Smackler snapped, "Dammit, Baldy, when you gonna learn to shoot?"

Contreas had been cleaning his Springfield muzzleloader and the ramrod was still in the barrel as he calmly poured a full load of powder in the pan, slipped a cap on the nipple and walked to where Sawyer lay thrashing in agony. He fired the ramrod completely through the man's body, burying it a foot deep in the ground beneath him.

"Ah, God!" Sawyer screamed, and went limp.

CJ stared at his brother. "You damned animals. You ain't soldiers. You're killers in uniform."

"Save him until last," Smackler said.

Birch walked over and looked at Jimmie Watson and asked Smackler, "What about the kid?"

"We'll take him on back to the camp. Send him to Fredericksburg," the sergeant said as he tossed a heavy hair rope up and over an outthrust limb.

John Smart was the first to die. They dragged him to the tree where he stood with the rope around his neck mumbling prayers. Two men slowly pulled him off his feet and, as his horrified friends watched, left him to kick and slowly strangle to death. When the body was finally still, they lowered it, cut the rope, leaving the loop deeply embedded in the victim's neck, and flipped the remainder back over the limb.

Staring up at the loop as it was lowered, Thayre, the second victim, suddenly screamed, "Major, you can't let this happen!" and then the rope was pulled tight and he rose slowly off the ground, his toes twitching frantically in an effort to reach firm footing. It required almost five minutes for him to die, and as his body jerked and twitched, William Shumahe suddenly dropped to his knees with tears streaming down his cheeks and began to pray in a loud voice.

Looking at him disdainfully, Smackler snarled, "Jerk that damn psalm singer up next," and watched as they cut the rope from Thayre's swollen neck and heaved it over the limb for yet a third time.

Alexander had not moved from his position against the tree but stood watching, his eyes brooding pits of hell, a drop of drool leaking from the corner of his slack mouth.

The rope cut off Shumahe in midprayer and he died in less than two minutes.

Jack Whitmire, who had a wife and three small children at home, pleaded with Smackler to allow him to write them as he was dragged to the dangling rope.

"What, and allow you to pass a message?" Birch snarled. "Pull him to hell," he ordered, and Malone and Courtney, who were now manning the rope, jerked the man off his feet with such force his legs swung against the trunk of the oak tree. Whitmire wrapped them around the tree as the rope slowly choked him to death and finally, losing consciousness, dropped to the end of the hang noose and kicked feebly, then was still.

"Next," Smackler snapped.

Abbott came forward then, his face a white, horrified mask, and said, "Sergeant, you can't go on with this. We'll all be marked for life for this crime. It's murder, Sergeant. We'll all hang for it just as you are hanging these men."

A tall, dark-complected soldier from Georgia stepped up and said, "Sergeant Smackler, not even war can excuse this."

"Get the hell back there," Smackler snarled, drawing his .45. "I'll kill the first man to interfere."

Birch had also drawn his gun, and now he swung it to cover the troopers who had refused to take part in the gruesome proceedings.

They dragged Jake Kyle to the rope, and just before he was pulled to his doom the brash young cowboy shouted, "My kin'll kill everyone of you stranglers. You'll all . . . ugh!'' and he was jerked up in his turn and was soon dead.

When it came Old Man Vanwinkle's turn, he walked to the oak tree with dignity, suffered the rope to be placed around his neck, then looking into Smackler's eyes, said coldly, ''Go ahead, you murdering bastard,'' and was pulled up. CJ Sawyer followed and died amid horrible gagging sounds that caused Abbott to turn away, white-faced.

When it was over, the bodies were left lying about under the oak tree. Malone and Contreas stripped them of their boots, and Timkins, his face a study in greed, searched their pockets for cash, turning them inside out. He found a total of $156.

Buel Courtney tied the dead men's weapons, blankets and camping gear behind their saddles, and the troop, silent now, rode from the clearing with Smackler on point.

Alexander rode twenty feet off on the right flank, his head down on his chest, allowing his horse to pick its own way.

Jimmie Watson had been tied to a horse and now he rode along, his eyes fixed on Smackler's back with a queer intensity.

Vent looked at the Preacher and shook his head. ''That's about the worst thing I ever heard of, Preacher. Did the boy get away?''

''He got away,'' the Preacher said.

''Hell of a thing,'' Vent grunted.

The Preacher rose and tossed several sticks of wood on the fire. ''You'll get a chance to hear it firsthand if you hang around. Watson's riding to meet me now.''

''The hell you say? He hire you?''

The Preacher shook his head. ''No, he didn't hire me. I mentioned he's my nephew. The boy's now a man full growed. He's a debt to settle, but he needs help settling it. I agreed to give him a hand.''

"He was sixteen then?'' Vent asked.

"Yep. He'd be thirty-five now. Ain't seen him since he was a baby in his mother's arms.''

"Now he wants to go after the men who hung his friends?'' Vent asked.

"That's about it,'' the Preacher agreed.

"Reckon I'll hang around,'' Vent said, and went to his saddle and carried it beyond the flames, laid out his bed and was soon asleep.

Chapter 2

Gene Smackler kicked the mud from his boots on the lower step of his back porch, then pushed open the screen door leading into the kitchen. Glancing at his wife, he sat down and carefully removed his spurs, then hung them on a peg driven into the wall near the door. Next came the heavy chaps and finally the high-crowned Stetson. Turning back into the kitchen, he nodded toward a pot simmering on the big old kitchen range and asked, "That stew?"

Molly Smackler turned from the stove and smiling mischievously, walked into his arms and kissed him soundly just as their daughter, pigtails flying, came pounding through the house from the front porch.

"Paw, Maw, they's strangers acoming up the road," she blurted out breathlessly.

Smackler's face turned solemn as he went to the front room and pulled back the curtains. Standing there with his hand hard down on the butt of the heavy Remington conversion model .36-caliber five-shot, he watched the two horsemen ride up and stop twenty feet from the wide veranda.

"Hello, the house," one of them called, and Smackler walked to the front door, picked up a Remington 44.40 rifle and cautiously pushed the door open, standing well clear of it.

"Name yourselves," he called.

One of the men looked at the other, then cleared his throat and called, "We're looking for Gene Smackler. This here where he lives?"

"Name yourselves, I said," Smackler countered.

"Name's Pete Jolly. Feller with me's Buel Courtney."

Carefully Smackler slid around the doorjamb and scrutinized the riders, then stepped boldly onto the porch and grinned. "Buel, I'd know that turkey neck anywhere." He laughed. "Go put your horses in the barn and come on in. We're about to set to table."

Jolly and Courtney dismounted and came to the steps where they solemnly shook Smackler's hand, then led their animals to a trough serviced by a creaking windmill and allowed them to bury their noses in the cool water.

When they came in the house a few minutes later, Smackler and Molly were standing in the kitchen door. Molly smiled at them and said, "Howdy, boys. It's been a lot of years, now ain't it?"

The couple's daughter, just turned fifteen and still a tomboy, stuck her head around the doorjamb and asked impudently, "Who're these fellers, Maw?"

Putting an arm around her, Molly said, "They served with your paw in the war."

The meal was a silent one, and once over, the men walked to the front porch and took chairs, nursing hot cups of coffee and long cigars provided by Courtney.

"Been a long time, Sarge," Jolly said. He was a small, tough-looking man with a beet-red complexion and eyes too close together. His hands never seemed to stay in one place, and Smackler watched them in fascination as they wandered up and down his shirtfront, onto the butts of his twin .45s and back to his too-tight collar, then fluttered on upward to cock his hat forward, then back again five minutes later.

Buel Courtney was a handsome man with long curly hair, a neatly trimmed mustache and clear blue eyes. Smackler recalled he had been the beau of suds row at Camp Verde and had become embroiled in several fights over the wives of some of the men who served there. Thinking about it now, the ex-sergeant also remembered Courtney was very fast with a handgun. Rumor had it he had killed half a dozen men in shoot-outs before joining the Confederate Army. The only man who ever challenged him at Camp Verde was a drifter who got likkered up in Bandera. He called Courtney a dude and, when the rattler-quick Texan knocked him down, drew his gun. Courtney punched his big ace.

Watching him now, Smackler thought how very few men would read the Texan's pedigree, passing him off for a flash gunman, partly due to the tony gun rig he affected. It was flower-stamped and decorated with Indian jade and hammered silver, as was his hatband. The gun was one of the new Lightning Colts, a .38 double-action first manufactured in 1877.

Smackler looked at Jolly and smiled. "It's been a long time. How'd you boys find me?"

Buel glanced up as Molly came around the house carrying a water pail and went to the windmill, where she hung the bucket on a spigot and pumped it full. The Texan's eyes gleamed and he ran his tongue around his lips as the woman bent over the water trough and lifted the bucket from the spigot, the effort pushing her full breasts hard into the thin cloth of her dress.

Smackler did not miss the look on Courtney's face.

Jolly, who had also been watching Molly, cleared his

throat and said, "Ran into Contreas in Tombstone. He's a deputy sheriff down there. Got hisself quite a little rep, he has. . . ."

"That figures," Smackler mused. "Saw him on the San Carlos River about a year ago. Told him I was over here."

Gazing absently out across the dry sagebrush, Courtney observed, "A hell of a place to wind up."

"Better than a stretched neck or a bullet in the brisket," Smackler said.

Courtney shook his head. "Hell, man, them days is long forgotten. That there was the war. Folks knows soldiers does all kinds of things in wars they wouldn't do otherwise."

Smackler grinned. "If you had it to do over again, you wouldn't hesitate one damn minute, Buel, and you know it."

"They was damn Yankees, that's what they was," Courtney insisted.

Jolly cleared his throat. "You hear about Malone?"

Smackler shook his head.

"Plugged. Law put him down at New Braunfels when he elected to hold court right smack dab in the middle of the street and went to the gun," Jolly said.

"Ted Hunnacker pushed in his chips up near Helena, Montana, in sixty-seven," Smackler said. "Hoss rolled on him. Working for the Hashknife, they tell me . . ."

Jolly shook his head. "Andy Belknap, he's blind. Got in a shooting scrape in Denver. Some gunsel cut down on him with a scattergun. Missed him complete but for two little pellets. When the smoke cleared away, old Andy couldn't see the tip of his own gun barrel."

"Ed Canto died in the spring of eighty," Courtney volunteered.

"The hell," Smackler said. "What took him away?"

"Doc didn't know. I was over near Nogales when I got

word he was about gone. Rode three nights and days and got there in time to throw on the last shovelful.''

Jolly looked around at the mean spread and asked, ''How come you to wind up here in New Mexico?''

''Come'n west. Stopped at Kelly to rest the horses. Feller offered to sell me this spread for four hundred dollars. I bought it.''

Courtney curled his lip. ''Should of shot the bastard.''

Smackler ignored him. ''Where you boys headed?''

Courtney grinned and, nodding toward Kelly, said, ''Figure on robbing the damn bank over there . . . that is iffin they got anything besides chicken feed in it. Reckoned you could tell us that.''

Smackler stared at him. ''Dammit, Buel, you gonna get every damn law west of the Mississippi down on me, you do that. Besides, that tin-can bank ain't got five dollars gold in it. Folks around here, they's so damn poor they deal in barter 'stead of money.''

''We heard a lot of big ranchers use that bank,'' Jolly said eagerly.

Smackler shook his head disgustedly. ''How come you fellers walkin' outside the law? Hell, you was wild but you wasn't crazy.''

''You been back to the South?'' Jolly asked.

''Never went back,'' Smackler said.

''You should have,'' was all Jolly said before standing up. He walked to the rail and looking at Smackler out of his mean eyes, added, ''You at least got you a home and a woman. We ain't got nothin'.''

Courtney stood up too, smiling his soft smile. ''You oughta know, they's word along the line that that kid we let go at Bandera is out hunting us.''

Smackler stared at him, then said disgustedly, ''I knew we should have stretched that brat's neck. Damn bushwhacker.''

"He ain't alone," Courtney said, and the tone of his voice caught all of Smackler's attention.

"Who's with him?" he asked.

Courtney looked at the barn then back at Smackler. "You make the best of that wife of yourn 'cause I got me a feeling ain't none of us gonna get out of this one."

"Dammit, never mind Molly!" Smackler snapped, standing up. "Who's with that kid?"

"For one thing, he ain't no kid no more," Jolly said.

"Turns out his uncle is a feller they call the Preacher. Ever hear of him?"

Smackler grunted, "Hell yes. Most everybody's heard of that gent. Only thing, I thought he was long dead. Why man, he must be eighty years old."

"Pretty close to it," Courtney said.

"Nothing to worry about," Smackler dismissed him.

Courtney smiled. "I couldn't beat him."

Smackler stared at him. "You've got to be joshin' me. . . ."

"No josh, Gene. That old boy's as fast as he ever was and the man siding him could spot us all two seconds and kill us without having to dodge even one of our bullets."

"Who the hell's with him, Doc Holliday?" Smackler asked sharply, not liking where this was going.

"Nope, feller named Leatherhand," Courtney said, and it was obvious he took a perverse pleasure in the announcement, even though the menace was his too.

"Leatherhand!" Smackler exclaimed. "But why him? Don't tell me he's some shirttail kin of that boy—"

"No kin, just a riding pard of the Preacher," Jolly put in.

"Damn." Smackler went to the veranda and looked toward Kelly. "You fellers really gonna hit the bank over there?"

"I reckon," Courtney said.

"Count me in. Looks like I need some running money."

Glancing at the house, Courtney asked, "What about her?"

"She'll be where I want her, don't worry," Smackler said, then added sourly: "If they plug me, you can come on back and help yourself, seeing as how you seem to fancy her so much."

"I might just do that." Courtney walked down the steps toward the barn as Smackler called for his daughter.

"Sissy, go saddle my black, will you?"

The girl came out and walked with Jolly to the barn where she threw the rigging on a big Morgan with powerful shoulders and long legs.

"See your paw still likes good horses," Jolly observed.

"Yes sir, he loves good horses," she answered, adding, "and so's his daughter" as she leaped on the animal's back and raced it to the front of the house where she came to a sliding, gravel-tossing stop.

"Kid's as loco as her paw," Jolly muttered.

"Gonna be a handful for some man real soon now," Courtney said.

Jolly stared at him. "You know, Buel, someday some feller is just naturally gonna haul off and fill your carcass plumb full of lead over that kinda talk."

"They's them that's tried it," Courtney said, staring hard at Jolly.

"Let's ride," Jolly said, refusing to return the look.

Baldy Birch grinned around his cigar at the bartender, then picked up his straight shot of old gravedigger and kicked it back, swallowing without making a face, and set the glass down on the mahogany bar.

"Damn good gullet grease," he said, and the thin bartender smiled and moved down the plank to wait on a noisy bunch of riders in from one of the big ranches over in the Smokey Hills country and hell bent on blowing a month's pay.

Lifting his gaze, he allowed his off-brown eyes to follow the undulating walk of one of the wine and dance girls
as she moved from table to table in search of a likely
customer. Apparently sensing Birch's eyes on her, she
turned and looked at him in the mirror. He winked and
watched her hesitate, then come over.

Leaning on the bar next to him, looking at him quietly
in the mirror, she allowed one of her full breasts to brush
his arm.

"You want a drink, lady?" he asked.

"Wine's fine." She smiled and the bartender poured the
drink.

"How much?" Birch asked bluntly, and now his eyes
shone sharp and brittle in the light from the overhead
lamps.

The girl looked at the floor for a moment, then looked
up at him in the mirror again and said softly, "Three
dollars," and gulped her drink.

"Let's go." He followed her up a stairway near the
back of the room.

He tramped after her along a hallway, and when she
stopped and put a key to a door, he moved up against her
and began caressing her hips. Pushing his hands away, she
said, "Three dollars . . . remember?"

Grinning his flat grin, he dug out a roll of bills and
followed her inside. Handing her three crumpled dollars,
he turned and locked the door, then looked out the window
into the alley.

She watched him quizzically, her head cocked to one
side, her eyes half closed. Somewhere down along the
main drag of this Kansas town of Hays, a wild Rebel yell
tore across Birch's consciousness, and he wheeled from
the window and walked over to the woman, stood very
close to her and asked, "What's yere name, missy?"

"Mae," she said, and her voice carried almost no

emotion, a good match for the quiet, expressionless eyes that looked inside him.

"Well, Mae, I reckon you and me, we're gonna get along just fine," Birch promised, and reaching out, he grasped the front of her dress and with a quick jerk bared both her full breasts.

She remained motionless, the cigarette in her mouth sending forth its tiny curl of smoke undisturbed.

Reaching out he put both hands on her and said softly, "Ahhh . . ."

She loosened the knot of her sash and let her dress fall, stepped clear of it and, shrugging away from his hands, went to the bed and lay down, the cigarette still in her mouth.

Riders rushed along the street below, the hooves of their horses hammering against the night, then four shots boomed slapping echoes against the side of the hotel and Birch turned his head and carefully checked the door, then moved to the bed and removed his clothes.

As he settled onto the hard mattress and pulled her against him, he said softly, "Feller never realizes until it's there in front of him . . ."

When he finally rose up and away from her, she did not move, but remained sprawled on the sheets, a smear of sweat on her upper lip and her eyes half closed.

Dressed, he turned and moved up beside the bed, then suddenly lashed out viciously, breaking her nose with the first blow and her cheekbone with the second. His third blow knocked out three teeth, and as she rolled unconscious onto the floor, he drove a boot toe into her ribs and giggled when he heard them crack. He searched a chest of drawers until he found a roll of bills, stuffing them into his pocket without bothering to count them. Then he walked to the alley window, lifted it and checked below, saw no one and moved out onto a landing, taking the stairs onto the street two at a time, humming to himself as he went.

When he reached the opposite side of the street, he
ambled along past L. Judd's Real Estate and Insurance
business and turned into the City Meat Market, where he
handed over one of the prostitute's soiled dollar bills for a
large hunk of German sausage and a loaf of bread. Back
on the street, he walked another half block, chewing on
the food as he dodged other strollers, then cut over to the
livery barn and emerged five minutes later astride a heavy-
chested bay gelding.

Several men glanced at him as he passed, noting the
low-hung gun on his left hip and the heavy-caliber rifle
thrust into a rifle boot beneath the skirt of his saddle. He
rode with hat tipped forward and shoulders back, ignoring
the glances.

He was two miles south of town when the bartender of
the saloon he had just left began to wonder where Mae was
and sent another girl in search of her. The second girl's
scream brought a dozen drinkers plunging up the stairs.
When they saw the girl's horribly damaged face, curses
ripped along the hall and down the stairs.

"Kicked her face in, he did," a waddy with Texas
written all over him said disgustedly.

"Anybody see the feller?" another man, a townsman by
the looks of his rumpled suit, called.

"I seen him," the bartender offered. "Big feller wearing a handgun on his left hip. Tough-looking jasper . . ."

"You mean the baldheaded one?" a short, bandy-legged
rider asked.

"Yep, that's the feller. Took off his hat when he first
came in," the bartender said.

A man wearing an apron with a pair of shears and a
comb in a breast pocket pushed forward. "I know that
gent. That there's Baldy Birch."

"Baldy Birch? You sure?" someone called from along
the hall.

The question was interrupted by the sudden appearance of the doctor, a fuss-budget of a man who pushed everybody out of Mae's room and ordered the door closed. He was followed up the stairs by a youthful-looking deputy marshal wearing two guns and toting a shotgun.

"What's going on here?" he asked. "Who's been beat up?"

"Mae, she's had the billy hell beat out of her," a man volunteered.

Scowling, the deputy asked, "Who done it?"

Several men cried out at once. "It was Baldy Birch, Jim. He brung the gal up here and beat the hell out of her."

"Looks like he whaled away on her with somethin' else too." One of the men snickered, earning a mean look from the deputy that caused him to drop his eyes and turn away.

"Anybody see which way Baldy went?" the deputy asked.

"Headed south, Jim. Probably going back to his ranch," the barber guessed.

"Anybody wanta go with me?" the deputy asked, and, when no one volunteered, turned toward the stairs, muttering: "Damn bunch of lilly-livered cowards . . . I'll bring the bastard in by myself."

An hour later the young deputy turned a bend in the trail and pulled his horse up sharply as Birch rode from behind a stand of trees.

"You're under arrest, Baldy," the deputy called, his voice almost cracking in the process.

Birch sat with his big hands clasped over the saddle horn and grinned at the deputy. "Hell, Jim, you don't wanta go and do that. Me, I sure ain't in no mood to plug a deputy. Not today, I ain't."

"No need for that," the lawman said. "Just come on along with me."

"What's the charge?" Birch's eyes plainly showed their scorn for the man with the badge.

"Assault. You beat hell outa Mae up to the Railroad Saloon. . . . Why the hell would a feller do a thing like that, anyhow?"

The smile stayed on Birch's face as he said, "Me, I don't like females. They give me a sick stomach."

"Hell, I don't like cows either, but I don't go around beating the billy bejesus outen them. . . . Now you come along, Baldy, and don't give me no trouble. . . ."

"Ah to hell with it," Birch snapped, and his left hand dipped, came up and blossomed smoke and flame before the lawman realized he was being shot at.

Birch's first bullet tore through the man's neck and his second slammed into the deputy's back as he was somersaulted over the cantleboard of his saddle.

He was dead when he hit the ground.

Birch looked down at the body and sighed. "Now I gotta move on," he said, then snarled, "damn you anyway," and raised the gun and hammered two more bullets into the back of the deputy's skull, blowing away most of his face.

Birch rode south at a steady trot, knowing he was going to have to abandon his small one-blanket spread and not really giving a damn.

"Time to move on anyway, horse," he told the bay, and gigged the animal into a slow gallop.

"Hey, Sheriff!" Rudy Timkins called, his nose pressed against one of the steel bars that held him imprisoned in the Prescott jail.

When the sheriff ignored his call, Timkins began cursing in a slow monotone, then shouted for the sheriff again. The door between the cell block and the office opened and a huge barrel of a man stepped through. He was wearing a brace of Peacemaker .45s with eagles carved in the white bone handles, a tall white hat and a pair of Mexican-made butterfly boots. The huge spurs with the silver-dollar rowels adorning the heels jangled musically as the sheriff lumbered along the catwalk and stopped in front of Timkins' cell.

Glaring at the prisoner, he growled, "What the hell ails you now, Timkins? Seems as how you got more complaints than an old woman with the miseries."

"You'd have complaints too if you was about to be hanged for somethin' you never done," Timkins said.

The sheriff shook his head. "You tell that story to the old feller with whiskers when you get up to the pearly gates, but I don't reckon he'll believe you either."

Timkins walked to the narrow, barred window and, standing in a thin spear of sunlight that lanced the floor, shook his head. "Me, I done a lot of bad things in my life, but I never killed old man Claybourne."

A deputy stuck his head through the doorway and called, "Sheriff Bratton, trouble over at the Desert Cactus . . ."

As the sheriff turned to leave, Timkins called, "Hey, how about some writing things. I need to write my people . . ."

"I didn't know you could write," Bratton said, looking at him narrowly.

"What's that supposed to mean?"

"Hell, where'd a saddle tramp like you learn to write?"

Timkins refused to answer. Instead he turned back and gazed out the window where two men were busily building the scaffold he would die on in three days.

Chapter 3

The Appaloosa and the black stud were covered with the dust of travel as they rounded into the single street of Kelly, New Mexico, and trotted past the line of false-fronted business establishments fronting the splintered wooden walk.

Vent Torrey, tall in his saddle, his feet thrust hard down in a pair of tapaderoed stirrups, their long, tapered ends almost brushing the ground, made his careful inventory of each building: a billiard hall, a small eating establishment, a saddlery, a land claim office, three saloons, a place called the California Store and a bank.

It was this structure that drew Vent and the Preacher's attention. A knot of men were gathered on the sidewalk and in the street. As they drew nearer, Vent saw the bodies of two men sprawled limply in the dust. One of them lay near a water trough where a snorting horse pulled back on its reins, its eyes walled toward the still form. The second lay flat on its back directly opposite the door of the bank about ten feet out in the street. A shotgun, its barrel broken away for reloading, rested against the sidewalk.

Two spent shells caught the reflection of the noon sun as it beat down into the dust of the street, bounced off the dry board-and-bat walls of the buildings and here and there touched a glass windowpane and threw back a dash of glitter.

The Preacher glanced at Vent. "I reckon maybe Jim better make it in here before a posse rides out. Could get tangled up with them if this here's what it looks like."

"Bank robbery, I figure." Vent stopped at the water trough, glanced down at the dead man who appeared to be a clerk from the looks of his clothes, then allowed his horse to drop its head and drink.

The Preacher ranged up on the opposite side of the trough and allowed the stud to bury its nose, ignoring both the body and the sidewalk gathering.

A hard-looking man carrying a rifle and wearing an S&W Schofield .45, a gun that wasn't too popular among either outlaws or lawmen, walked out to the trough, took in the way Vent wore his .44 and the old man his twin .45s, and asked, "You fellers see anybody south of here?"

Vent pushed back his hat. He watched the man with the rifle follow the movement with his eyes and said, "Nope. Only the stage. It was heading down trail about half a day's ride from here."

"I'm the marshal . . . Name's Al Cooper. Been a bank holdup. Three fellers rode in and stuck her up. Rode off with more than fifty thousand they did."

The Preacher pushed his black hat to the back of his head, baring a silver mane of hair, and said doubtfully, "This here place don't look all that prosperous. Where the hell did that kind of money come from?"

Cooper looked around. "It don't look like much, but then we're getting there. Railroad's coming through here for sure. Town'll grow . . . Ranchers around here use this bank. Big outfits. Some of them fellers going to be riled about this . . .''

"You know any of the holdups?" Vent asked.

"Sure," the marshal said. "Big feller was Gene Smackler. Owns a one-blanket spread north of here. Sorry-lookin' outfit. 'Bout the only good-looking thing on it is his wife Molly.''

As they talked, a dark-complected rider wearing a white cavalry hat pinned up on the left side, a .45 Colt, heavy bullhide chaps and a vest made from the hide of a cougar, trotted a small, compact grulla into the main street. The marshal looked up keenly, shook his head and said softly, "We ain't had anybody visit here in over a year and now we got three visitors. . . ." He looked back at Vent and said, as if talking to himself, "Wonder what makes us so popular all of a sudden?''

The man on the grulla rode up to the trough, nodded at Vent and the Preacher, glanced at the two dead men and allowed his horse to drink. He hooked a leg around the narrow swell of the army McClelland saddle he rode and extracted tobacco and papers.

"Howdy, stranger," the marshal said.

"Howdy." The rider licked his cigarette closed and glanced at Vent. "Got a match, Mr. Torrey?''

Vent was watching the marshal. When the man on the grulla used his name, Cooper suddenly became watchful. Vent thought, He knows who I am, and handed the rider a match, nodded at Cooper and said, "This here gent's name is Jim Watson. I'm Vent Torrey and the mean-looking one is the Preacher.''

A man wearing a deputy sheriff's badge had walked over just before Vent made his introductions and now he looked up at Vent and said, "Name's Had Putnam. County law in this neck of the woods. You fellers passing through?''

Watson looked around with an expressionless face. "Hell

no, Deputy, we're fixing to start us a two-story, block-long mercantile right smack dab on the edge of your town.''

Putnam tried on a smile for size and the effort was just a bit feeble, Vent noted, and wondered if he too had recognized them.

Cooper sat the rifle down butt first. "Feller robbed the bank was sided by a coupla gents looked like trouble on the run.'' He pointed down toward the livery. "I was just coming from the livery when they ran from the front door. The horses was tied right there in front. They just hopped on and headed for the end of town. That's when Mert and Wiley come bustin' out throwing lead all over the landscape.''

"Was you throwing lead?'' Watson asked.

Cooper looked sheepish as he said, "I wasn't wearing my gun. Took it off to clean my horse's stall and the damn thing was still hanging from a stall stanchion.''

"Happens,'' the Preacher said.

Cooper threw a grateful look at him, then said, "Those fellers riding with Smackler . . . They was new around here. One good-looking gent wearing a real tony gun rig and carrying one of them newfangled Lightning double-actions . . . Mr. Brown, he's the president of the bank, he spotted the gun. Said he had just sent for one he saw in the catalogue. Knowed what they looked like.''

Watson glanced at Vent. "This man have curly hair and blue eyes . . . Look like a Texan?''

"That's him all right. The clothes was Texican . . .''

"Buel Courtney,'' Watson said, and his face was a hard mask.

The deputy pushed his hat back on his head and said softly, "Heard of him. Gunman, ain't he?''

Vent looked down street, then brought his gaze around to Putnam. "Some might think so.''

"The other feller . . . What kinda looking gent was he?" Watson asked.

Vent had been watching the group standing near the bank, and as Cooper described the third man as a "tough-looking hombre with a lot of hard bark on him and the meanest little eyes I ever did see," a tall, dignified towns-man came over and asked quietly, "You plan on getting up a posse, Had?"

Watson said, "Pete Jolly. That's the third man."

The townsman looked up sharply and then carefully examined the three mounted men. "You men lawmen?" he finally asked.

"Not now," Vent said. "Have been."

"Just interested parties," Watson added, dropping his used-up cigarette into the dust and lifting his leg over the swell of the McClelland and anchoring his boot in the metal stirrup. "Best move along, fellers, while we still got light to track by."

"Wait a minute, men, I'd like to make you a proposi-tion," the townsman said, looking at Vent.

"This here's Thaddeus Brown, the banker," Putnam said, and at that moment a young woman came from the bank and walked to Brown. Keeping her eyes averted from the sprawled bodies, she took the bank president's arm and said, "Daddy, they got away with over fifty thousand dollars . . . those damned thieves," and then her face grew red as she looked up and caught Vent staring at her.

"My daughter," Brown said wryly. "Name's Angel . . . don't ask me why. It was her maw's idea."

Vent nodded gravely. The Preacher removed his hat, smiled, and Vent was reminded of a trapped lobo wolf he had once run to ground. Watson smiled, said, "Ma'am," and looked away.

Putnam made the introductions: "This here's Vent Torrey, and this gentleman is called the Preacher. The young feller's name is Jim Watson,'' and looking up at Vent, he asked: "You said you were a lawman once?"

"Marshaled at Creed, Colorado, and a couple of other places," Vent said.

Suddenly the deputy's eyes grew wide as he stared at the leather glove on Vent's gunhand. "Leatherhand, by God." Brown and his daughter both looked startled as they turned their eyes on Vent's hand.

"I shoulda knowed when you said that gent was called the Preacher," Putnam declared, pointing at the old man, who sat carefully trimming the end from a cigar.

Cooper looked at Putnam and grinned. "Hell fire, Had, I thought you knew who they were."

"Too busy worrying about this damned holdup," the deputy said, then glanced at Angel and her father. "These fellers would sure make for a bangup posse, Mr. Brown. . . ."

A lanky man wearing a pair of bib overalls and runover flat-heeled boots came over, and Vent thought, This feller has sodbuster written all over him, and waited to see what he had to offer.

"Mr. Brown, us fellers been talking this over and we figure that unless you get that there money back, why Kelly will die where she sits."

Watson declared, "What the hell ever give anybody the idea this here lashup was alive and breathing?"

"Who're you?" the farmer asked.

Watson looked at him and said lazily, "I'm a Texican, and that should be enough for you, friend."

"The hell you say?" the farmer retorted pugnaciously.

Watson looked at Vent, then casually drew his gun and pointed it at the farmer's head. "You want I should put her through your head or in the gut?" He let the barrel sag until it bore on the man's stomach.

The farmer, his face white, turned to the marshal and squealed, "Hey now, Al, you're the law here. Do some-

thing before this yahoo shoots me. . . . Hell, look at him
. . . he's crazy, he is. . . .''

"Ain't crazy," Watson avowed. "Just never liked
sodbusters."

Putnam, who had spent enough time around Texans,
knew he was seeing a sample of that breed's idea of a
joke, and it showed all over his face. Vent wondered how
long he would stand there and let Watson horraw the
farmer.

"Put that gun away, you idiot," Angel Brown suddenly
snapped. "Hasn't there been enough killing here?"

Watson glanced at her and smiled. "In Texas, we don't
call shooting sodbusters killing. It's kinda like getting rid
of loco weed or bumping off a sick cow."

"Very funny," she replied, staring up at Watson, eyes
snapping and mouth a straight line of disapproval.

Looking at her, Watson told Brown, "You're right. She
ain't no angel."

Brown chuckled, then apparently having recognized
horrawing when he was faced with it, put an arm around
Angel and said, "Shucks, baby, he's just funnin'."

"Some fun," she sniffed, and, back straight as a ramrod,
marched back inside the bank.

Vent was sorry to see her leave. He had been quietly
looking at her during Watson's game with the farmer and
had liked what he saw. She had dark, wavy hair that hung
past her shoulders, a fine-boned face with rather high
cheekbones and a delicate, flaring nose. Her eyes were
bigger than usual and a brilliant green. When she was
angry, as she had been while confronting Watson, they
flared and sparked. Vent guessed her height at about five
two or three, but because she had been dressed for riding
in a pair of high-heeled boots and split skirt, it was hard to
tell. The fact that she was fairly well endowed was quite

obvious, in spite of the rather loose checkered shirt she was wearing, and added to her attractiveness.

"Mr. Slattery here owns a thousand acres west of town and raises almost all the hay around," Brown said, nodding at the farmer, who was still under Watson's gun.

Shrugging, Watson holstered the big .45. Digging out the makings, he observed, "Reckon I cain't shoot a feller who raises hay for cows and horses. My apologies, Mr. Slattery," and he deftly rolled a smoke, offered the farmer the sack and grinned when he accepted it.

Brown, meanwhile, had been looking over Vent and his friends' horses, apparently noting the sweat-streaked trail dust on them, and now he said, "Those horses look to me like they could use a rest, a rubdown and some grain and time to eat it. We have a good livery here and a better-than-average café if you gents will join me. I may have lost fifty grand but I've still got the price of a meal, and if I ain't, then Mick over at the Kelly Emporium will certainly extend me credit."

Watson looked doubtful, but Vent, knowing the banker was right, merely nodded and dropped from the saddle. The Preacher and Watson followed.

After taking care of the horses, they met the banker in front of the café; he had his daughter and Putnam with him.

Seated at a large table near the back of the half block-long room, they ordered steak, potatoes, fried eggs and a huge pot of coffee. No one spoke during the meal, but twice when Vent looked up, he caught the girl's eyes on him, and although their green depths showed him nothing of the thoughts behind them, he knew she was curious.

The meal over, they sat back with full coffee cups and Angel asked Vent, "Is it true, Mr. Torrey, all the stories we hear about you?"

"What kind of stories are you referring to, Miss Brown?"

Vent asked, noting a faint smile on the Preacher's normally expressionless face. The old coot, he thought, as she replied, "They say you go about shooting folks. . . ."

"I have shot men," he admitted.

"Many?" she pressed.

"I stopped counting after the first one," Vent told her, and a coldness had crept into his voice.

Brown cleared his throat. "You'll have to forgive my daughter, sir, she has more curiosity than discretion. Not her fault. A family trait."

Watson cocked his head and raised an eyebrow. "Lose many of your family that way?"

Brown grinned faintly. "As a matter of fact, Mr. Watson, several, but I hope Mr. Torrey is gentleman enough to spare my daughter. She's the only one I have."

"Your daughter has nothing to worry about," Vent assured him. "I don't make war on women . . . even overly curious ones."

During this interchange, Angel had sat staring straight at Vent and her level green gaze made him uncomfortable.

Brown nodded. "Appreciate that," and there was a twinkle in his eye when he said it. "Now, I would like to make a proposal. You gentlemen apparently came to Kelly for a reason. It's off the regular trail routes, there isn't much to attract three men of your caliber, so I figure you are after Smackler and his men. . . . Am I right?"

Vent tore his eyes away from Angel's unblinking stare and said, "We're looking for them, all right, but not for anything they did recently. This here's a personal quarrel between Mr. Watson and Smackler and his pards."

Glancing at Watson, who was looking out the dust-streaked front window and toying with his cup, Brown asked, "Mr. Watson, you willing to include our problem with yours?"

Watson turned cold eyes on the banker. "No matter.

Smackler, Courtney and Pete Jolly are dead men. If we happen to retrieve your money in the process, we'll see that it comes home.''

"I'll pay a five-thousand-dollar reward for its return," Brown said.

Watson shook his head. "Mr. Brown, I own half a million acres of Texas ground and run over a hundred thousand head of prime beef. I got so damn many horses I've lost count and, in fact, my segundo says they have foals faster than he can count them. I don't need money. As I told you, I'll return your fifty grand if it's still in these fellers' hands when we lay them down."

"You just gonna kill them?" Putnam asked.

"Just gonna kill them," Watson agreed.

"But why?" Angel asked. "They should be returned for trial."

Watson hesitated for just a moment, then said, "You've heard of the Bandera hills massacre? That was Smackler, Courtney, Jolly and a few others. . . ."

Brown stared at him, then said softly, "Of course. Watson. I understand now. . . . But, Mr. Watson, they said you'd been murdered by those fellows."

"They didn't murder me. They sent me to Fredericksburg instead." Watson's voice was cold.

Putnam shook his head. "How old were you, Mr. Watson?"

"Sixteen, and scared plumb to death. I never figured them to let me go. Why they didn't just hang me with the rest I'll never know."

"That was a terrible black mark on the South," Brown said.

"It was, when you consider my nephew was in sympathy with the South," the Preacher, who had been sitting listening quietly, said.

"Your nephew?" Angel asked.

"Yes, Miss Brown, Jim's my nephew."

"Well, my offer still holds. I'll pay five thousand dollars for the return of the money those men robbed," Brown said.

They left the café and stood on the sidewalk as a lifting wind came pushing out of the north, bringing an ominous promise of a storm with it. Balls of sage rolled along the street, frightening horses at hitchracks and tumbling beneath porch stoops, where they lodged with others that had rolled there during earlier storms.

Vent looked off to the northwest and, seeing a huge cloud bank building far into the sky like a giant pillar of cotton, said, "Looks like we're in for a rough one."

Putnam looked at the clouds. "We don't get storms here very often, but when we do, they tear the hell outa things. Reckon I better go help the folks get shutters up." Vent noticed men and women hurrying onto porch stoops with boards under arms and hammers in hand.

As the storm kept building, Vent and his friends took a hand, helping the little town button up for what was coming. Half an hour later, they sat in the closed and shuttered bank and listened to the climbing howl of the wind. Angel sat stiffly, hands clasped in her lap and eyes closed, listening as the storm roared into Kelly like the mill tails of hell, hurling loose boards against the sides of the bank with a loud clatter and driving puffs of dust beneath the doors and around the window jambs.

Brown hurried to a storeroom and came back with a bundle of rags. Vent and Putnam helped him stuff cracks, but the dust still found its way inside.

Somewhere a tin chimney tore loose from the roof of a house and clattered loudly each time it touched down on some obstruction. It finally blew through the partially open haymow door of the livery and landed in the hay piled there, scaring the wild-eyed horses in the process. A stable hand climbed the rickety ladder and fought the wind in an effort to close the door as Vent watched through a crack alongside a window. Suddenly the man was snatched into the open, still clinging to the haymow door, which in turn slammed against the side of the building with a loud bang that echoed down the street above the rushing sound of the storm. The unfortunate stable hand, still clinging to the upper edge of the door, was slammed twice more into the side of the barn as Vent watched.

Turning, he hurried to the front door and shouted at Watson, ''Close this behind me, Jim,'' and was gone before anyone could object.

Out on the sidewalk he was forced to grab a porch support to keep from being blown over. Hanging on against the powerful surge of the wind, he braced himself, bending over to cut down wind surface, and made it to the corner of the first street only to run straight into a powerful crosscurrent that knocked him off his feet and dumped him unceremoniously on his back. He managed to regain his feet and, clinging to whatever obstruction offered itself, reached the livery barn, but then was forced to drop flat against the side of the building to avoid being struck by several boards that had apparently been ripped from a house somewhere and came sailing straight at him, jagged ends first. They smashed into the side of the barn and Vent was amazed to see two of them actually penetrate the board-and-bat siding and disappear half their length inside the livery.

A faint cry from above galvanized him into action as he looked up and saw the stable hand still dangling twenty feet above the street. Sliding along the wall with the wind pinning him, he finally made the big double doors but hesitated to open one. Then he saw a smaller door, jerked it open, dived inside as the wind ripped it from his hand and slammed it into the side of the inner wall.

As the horses suddenly began lunging and squealing, he got behind the door and slowly forced it closed. Grabbing a rope from one of the saddles, he literally ran up the ladder to the loft and made his way through the wildly swirling hay to the door. Building a loop, he hurled it toward the man, only to watch it stop in midair as if it had struck an invisible wall, then blow back straight out behind him like a giant snake. Cursing, Vent brought the rope back to him as the man turned a frightened face and shouted something.

Vent shook his head, then the man shouted again, and Vent heard the word "pitchfork" and quickly went in search of one. When he found it, only the tip of the handle was visible above the piles of hay, blown into miniature mountains by the savage winds. Running back to the door, Vent slowly worked the handle out toward the man and watched as he made his grab for it one-handed. He marveled at the stable hand's strength as he still clung to the door with one hand and clutched the pitchfork handle with the other.

Using most of his own strength, Vent managed to draw the door back to him, and as it passed the center mark, the wind suddenly pushed it savagely inward; when it struck, the stable hand was tossed loose and dumped ten feet inside the barn as Vent grabbed the doorknob. With the wind gone, the hay began to drift down all over the barn.

"Mister, that was one hell of a chance you took," the stable hand said. "You could have got killed out there," and as if to emphasize his words, the wind hurled something big against the building, shaking its very foundations.

"This here's worse than a Texas tornado," Vent shouted, and then he noticed the man's bleeding hands and leaned over and yelled in his ear: "Let's go downstairs. Should clean that up and get some cow grease on it."

Half an hour later the storm suddenly withdrew its

howling clamor, and it grew so quiet Vent wondered if anybody in the town was left alive. Opening the wide doors, he stepped into the street as businessmen all along the main drag came hesitantly from their shops to stand and stare in wonder at the ripped boards, bent stovepipes and smashed buckets that littered the street and alleys.

Walking to the bank, Vent was in time to meet Brown and Angel. "How's the liveryman?" Brown asked.

"Hands peeled up a bit, but he'll do. Tough feller."

"That took nerve, Mr. Torrey," Brown said.

Vent did not answer but merely nodded, and then the Preacher and Watson came up. "Let's ride," he said, and, shaking Brown's hand, went to the livery to saddle the spooky Appaloosa.

As they rode past the bank, Vent noticed Angel was nowhere in sight and wondered about it, but then waved at Brown as Putnam stepped from the sidewalk. "If you fellers have no objection, I'd like to ride along. . . ."

"No objection," Vent said.

"I'll get my horse," the deputy replied, and hurried toward the livery.

While they waited for the lawman, the marshal came along the street, looking at the wreckage and shaking his head, "Damn storm tore the hell outa everything," he said.

"Anybody hurt?" Vent asked.

"No, nobody hurt," Cooper answered. "Folks around here are used to these damn storms. Anybody who lives in this part of the country knows they ain't nothing between here and the north pole but a barbed-wire fence, and it's down. They just kinda expect to get blowed all over the prairie about three times a year."

Putnam rode up then and said, "I'm going along with these boys. Maybe we'll get lucky and run up on Smackler before he plunges all the bank's money over a card table."

"What about Molly Smackler?" Cooper asked. "You want me to bring her in and question her?"

Putnam shook his head. "No need for that. She'd just tell you to go to hell or blink them big eyes at you and that'd be the end of it."

Cooper grinned. "Just thought I'd ask."

"Tamp her light," Putnam counseled, and followed Vent and his friends out of town.

Five miles south of town, Angel Brown rode a blaze-faced sorrel from a cut in the prairie and reined in beside Vent. "I'm heading south. Could use an escort."

"Your daddy know you're here?" Watson asked.

"He knows." She leveled her green eyes on him.

"Just keep your head down when you're told to," Vent said, and rode on.

"Does anything reach him?" Angel asked the Preacher, whose stud was sniffing at the sorrel's flank.

"Not that I ever saw," the Preacher said, and jerked the black's head up and moved him away from the girl's horse.

"Damn stud acts like every man I ever met," she said, and now there was a sparkle in her eyes.

Seven days had passed and Vent wondered if they were any closer to Smackler and his men than the day he led his little posse away from Kelly.

Turning in his saddle, he looked back at the Preacher, who sat bolt upright on his big stallion and rode in stolid silence. Behind him Had Putnam, clothes covered with trail dust and eyes red from the blowing sand, sat dozing on the back of his horse. Jim Watson rode with one foot dangling free of the stirrup and eyes scanning each bit of cover they passed. His rifle lay across the swell of his saddle and he kept his right hand hard down on it. Angel Brown met his eyes and tried a smile on for size. It was weak, but Vent gave her a high mark for the effort.

They had trailed the Smackler gang from Kelly south for ten miles, when the line of tracks cut sharply west, leading them through a narrow pass in the Magdalena Mountains, then by another pass that zigzagged through the San Mateo Mountains and finally over the Mogollon Mountains. Once clear of the Mogollons, Smackler's bunch had cut sharply south again and skirted the southern edge of the Apache reservation then broke north.

Each night for eight nights, they camped in the desert, or in some dark cut in the mountains. A stop had been made at Piños Altos, a mining town, where they bought grub at a general store constructed of lumber so new the pitch was still being boiled from it by the hard heat of the New Mexico sun.

The store clerk said he had sold three hard-looking men several boxes of ammunition and a bait of grub. "They went across the street to the Silver Dollar and took on some liquid nerve, then stopped at the livery and bought half a sack of grain and rode out."

When Vent thanked him, he looked at Putnam and asked, "Ain't you Had Putnam from over Kelly way?"

Putnam nodded and the man said, "You chasing those fellers?"

"Reckon we are," Putnam told him. "They robbed the Kelly bank and killed a coupla gents."

The clerk shook his head and observed, "A hell of a thing. Hope you catch them."

They rode out and picked up the fleeing bank robbers' trail west of town. Vent had looked down at those tracks so long that he was beginning to see them in his sleep.

They hit Shakespeare just as the sun went down, and Vent noted the crowded sidewalks and the blaring music of rinky-dink pianos coming from half a dozen watering spas fronting the sidewalk. "Reckon it's time to rest the horses and get a good night's sleep. We'll put up here for the night.''

''Pretty wild-looking lashup,'' Watson observed, pulling his horse to one side to avoid two men who had crashed through the swinging doors of a saloon and were now mauling each other in the dust of the street.

Angel rode straight into and over them, and the two men howled and leaped to their feet, grabbing at her horse's reins.

Vent wheeled his horse sharply, rode in on top of the brawlers and, whipping his gun out, slammed one over the head. As he toppled into the dirt with a groan, Vent hit the second man and backwalked his horse to give the miner room to fall.

As he sheathed his pistol, a man dressed in black coat and gray trousers moved out from the shadows of a shoe repair shop and the glitter of silver hit by a light shaft signaled the man was law.

''Pretty rough treatment there, stranger,'' he said laconically.

''Street's no place to fight,'' Vent countered, and watched the man's hands.

The Preacher swung his horse around sharply and drew his .45. ''Come to hell outa there, hombre, or you're dead meat.'' A man cursed, then stepped into the open, rifle sagging toward the sidewalk. He too wore a badge.

''Hey now,'' the black-coated lawman said, and then Vent pushed his hat to the back of his head and the lawman drew in his breath and said to his partner, ''Easy now, Joe. Looks like we got the top layer in our town. . . .''

The second deputy moved out farther into the light. '' 'Pears to me like a bunch of pilgrims on the drift.''

The first lawman grinned wolfishly, then nodded toward Vent. ''Gent with the leather on his hand is Vent Torrey . . . Leatherhand. The gentleman in black is the Preacher.

You probably don't remember me, Preacher, but I saw you down in Pecos when them greasers jumped ya. I was the man riding the paint horse.''

"I remember," the Preacher said, but he still kept his gun in his hand.

Jerking a thumb toward the second lawman, the first lawman said, "This here's Joe Helger. My name's Rand Carpenter. I'm the marshal here," and Vent recalled then a story he had heard about this man and understood why the Preacher still fisted his gun.

Carpenter had once marshaled in Waco, Texas, and had had trouble with one of the big ranchers in the area. Hearing the outfit was on the way to town, Carpenter spread the story they were on their way to attack the marshal's office. He put together a posse and set up an ambush. When the rancher rode into town with six of his men, Carpenter gave the order and all seven cowboys died in the street without ever firing a shot.

"You boys passing through?" Helger asked.

"Plan to stay over until morning. Need a decent night's rest and so do the horses," Jim Watson said, and now the two men looked at the rancher, apparently trying to read his pedigree. Vent guessed the lawmen had Angel figured as the wife of one of them and chuckled inwardly.

Angel rode close to the sidewalk and said, "You men recommend a good hotel?"

"Certainly, ma'am." Carpenter removed his hat with a gallant flourish. "Two blocks down. The Shakespeare House. Best in town."

"Thank you." She turned and rode toward the far end of the street where the two-story hotel stood head high above the businesses surrounding it.

Vent followed her while the Preacher walked his horse sideways along the street, his gun still in his hand but pointing now at the ground. Putnam, rifle held casually across the saddle, smiled at the lawmen, observed, "Nice little town you fellers got here," and rode after the Preacher.

Vent caught up to Angel in time to hear her snap, "Now there's a deadbeat on the fly if I ever saw one. Feller's all gurgle and no guts."

Vent smiled.

As they rode slowly along the main street, Vent glanced up at the low hills surrounding this booming mining town and watched as dozens of men emerged from mine tunnels and shafts as the day shift ended and straggled down slope into the nearest saloon.

Angel reined her horse into the hitching rack and stepped lithely down, her face a set mask as she ignored the leers cast her way by the miners, each with his small lunch pail in hand and a powerful thirst in his gullet.

Vent turned in next to her and laid a level look at the loiterers and watched the eyes fall away as feet began to shuffle, then they moved off. The Preacher moved in beside Angel and reached and took her horse's reins and said, "I'll put away the animals while you folks hire us a room."

"Until we got more of an idea where these damn bank robbers are holed up, we better travel in pairs," Watson said as Putnam and the Preacher moved off.

Vent followed the girl inside and stopped at the desk as Watson checked the dining room.

"A room, folks?" the clerk asked.

"Nope," Vent replied. "Five rooms. And plenty of hot bathwater in each. You can start with the lady, and when the other boys get here, we'll see how fast you can get us taken care of."

Spinning the register, the clerk said, "Sign here, please," and Vent wrote Angel's name, then his own and the Preacher's and finally Watson's.

"How much?" he asked.

The clerk spun the register back again and glanced down at the names, then froze. Slowly he looked up at Vent and drew a deep breath. "That'll be . . . twelve dollars . . . Mr. Torrey, sir . . ."

Vent paid him and watched his trembling fingers dig out the keys, dropping two of them in the process.

"Keep two keys here and give me the other three," Vent said. "When a tall old feller wearing black comes in followed by a mean-looking jasper with guns and knives hanging all over him, you give them the other two keys."

The clerk swallowed and said, "Yes sir," and came around the counter. "This way, Mr. Torrey—ma'am," and started up toward the second floor just as Watson stepped around the corner and signaled Vent.

After Angel had gone on up, Vent retraced his steps and asked, "What's up, Jim?"

"Smackler. He and those two thugs, Courtney and Jolly, are sitting in the dining room acting as if they own it. All reared back, hats sitting on their damn necks, pistol butts just ashining and playing the bullyboys."

Just then Putnam and the Preacher came in from the street. They were halfway across the lobby when someone suddenly shouted, "Look out, it's that bastard, Putnam," and a gun crashed, sending a bullet screaming past the deputy's head to push a window into the street in an eruption of flying glass.

Vent whipped around the corner, took in the sight of Smackler, Courtney and Jolly with guns in their hands and went for his own gun. Then the Preacher acted. His .45s leaped into his hands as Vent fired. Knowing Smackler was the most dangerous of the three, Vent shot him through the face and watched clinically as the big .44 slug tore through the man's brainbox, blasting the back of his head back into the dining room to splatter a petrified waiter, who promptly hit the floor, sending his tray sailing away with a great clatter.

The Preacher's .45 roared and Jolly screamed, clutched his stomach and ran backward ten feet, was hit again, this time by Watson and Putnam, and spun around twice and collapsed with a moan.

Courtney had dodged clear of the door on the first shot and Vent dived through the opening, whirling toward the west side of the room just as the gunman disappeared behind a door leading to the alley. When Vent hit the door on the run, Watson was on his heels, and they burst into the alley, immediately leaping away from each other, guns swinging to cover east and west.

Nothing.

Then a cat howled as if someone had stepped on its tail and Vent whipped around a corner into a narrow walkway behind a line of businesses, shouting at Watson as he dodged into the opening, "Around the block, Jim. Let's cut him off," and heard the rancher's bootheels slamming down on the hard-packed ground as he passed the narrow aperture.

Gun in hand, Vent ran along the catwalk, his eyes automatically checking each opening as he came to it. He was three-fourths of the way along the narrow way when a shadow suddenly sprang from a recessed doorway and fired. Vent felt the savage rip of lead as it struck him somewhere in the leg, then he fired three times so fast the shots sounded as one.

The gunman screamed high and wild as he was driven backward by the triple blow to his chest. Then he smashed into the side of a building and rebounded to sprawl on his face in the dirt. As Vent limped forward, several doors swung open, sending beams of light spearing into the catwalk, then blinked out as the doors were hastily jerked shut.

Stopping five feet from his victim, Vent watched him narrowly, then noted the gleam of gun metal three feet from the sprawled figure's outstretched hand and decided he had fired his last shot.

Squatting on his heels, he looked into Courtney's face as the man's eyes slowly opened, regarded him with detachment, and then the gunman actually smiled.

Vent watched as the light died in the eyes and the smile turned into a grimace, followed by the rattle of Courtney's final breath. As he died, Watson strode up, stopped and had his look and observed, "Three down, four to go."

Chapter 4

Sheriff Bratton stood spraddle-legged on the high pinnacle and stared west to where a thin ribbon of dust trailed out a hundred yards behind a rider, then was whipped in a sharp curve to the south, and thought, He's got a good day on us, and wished he was back in Prescott sipping a tall beer.

Turning at the sound of loose rock rolling down slope, he watched Cat Kittle, his deputy, scramble up to the ridge top and said absently, "He's gonna be hell on little red wheels to come up on," and pointed.

Where Bratton was fat all over, Kittle was a tall, long-necked man with a weak chin and a walrus mustache. He wore his guns butt out because he had once seen a picture of Wild Bill Hickok wearing his pearl-handled sixes in a sash with the butts forward and had decided to follow the famous gunman's example. What surprised Bratton was that Kittle had actually improved his speed, somehow mastering the odd roll required to bring the guns into action.

"Hell, he's into Yavapia country now," Kittle said. "If we don't catch him, the 'Paches will."

''We'll get him,'' Bratton promised, but inside he wasn't that sure. Rudy Timkins was running from a hang rope and the sheriff knew there was no greater incentive to get shy of a country than the threat of a stretched neck.

''What gets my bile is that we had him almost up the steps to the scaffold,'' Kittle said, and rolled a cigarette.

''What you fellers doing up there? Fixin' to homestead?'' a red-headed rider squatting on the ground with several other men called up from the base of the low ridge.

''Naw,'' Kittle called. ''Del, he says he's gonna see if he can hit old Rudy from up here,'' and laughed hoarsely, ignoring Bratton's scowl.

Moving quickly for a big man, the sheriff turned and dropped down the steep slope, grunting when his butterfly boots sank almost to their mule ears in the soft sand. Kittle watched the distant rider for half a minute, then came down behind the sheriff, pulled the cinch tight on his horse and said, ''We should hit water on the Big Sandy if we don't run afoul a bunch of them damned hair-lifters first.''

''I ain't heard nothin' about no Apache raids lately,'' a stalky posse member said. Nobody answered.

Mounting, they moved down into the hot dish of desert, picking up the escapee's trail half a mile from the ridge. As the horses moved west at a shuffling trot, Bratton wondered how the hell Timkins had managed to get his hands on the piece of wire he had used to strangle Handy Cane, the jailer. After looking at Cane's swollen face and neck, Bratton vowed he would never quit until Timkins was either dead or swinging from the end of a rope, and looking at his hard-bitten posse, he figured he just might not get Timkins back to Prescott and didn't much give a damn. Cane's brother, Bill, had joined them as they rode from town. He was a quiet man who probably hadn't spoken two hundred words in the five years Bratton had known him, but he had a deadly reputation with the big

Sharps rifle he carried. They said of Bill Cane that if a fly moved its wings five hundred yards away, he could not only hear and see it, but hit it too. Bratton knew that if Bill Cane got a clean shot at Timkins, they could forget about bringing him back for a hanging.

That night, the posse made camp on the banks of the Big Sandy. Looking down at the shallow smear of water, Bratton was glad it was spring or he might have been looking at a dry riverbed. As he returned to the fire, one of the men said softly, "Iffin that varmint is playing Injun out there somewhere, we don't have to worry. He'll damn sure shoot at Del, him being the biggest target in this part of Arizona," and Bratton suddenly felt terribly exposed and moved out of the fire glow as the others chuckled.

Red Heep, the cowboy who had called to Bratton back at the ridge, pushed his hat back and reached for the coffeepot. He never heard the shot that sent the 38.40 slug tearing into his chest, knocking him sideways as the posse suddenly erupted into violent action.

One man cursed wildly and kicked dirt on the fire only to take a round through the leg for his bravery. Bratton had dropped behind a rock at the first shot and now he watched the opposite side of the river as the posse scrambled for cover.

Kittle crawled up beside him, both guns fisted, and growled, "That bushwhacking son of a bitch. He's sure as hell killed Red."

Then the rifle banged again and Bratton saw the flash of its powder charge and triggered three rapid shots at the telltale marker as the rest of the posse opened up a second later.

When they stopped shooting, it was dead quiet for a long moment, then the rifle suddenly sounded again, this time slamming out a string of shots so close on each other they blended in a slashing roar. Bullets ploughed into the

camping area, knocking the coffeepot spinning and burying one round in a saddletree with a loud thunk. Then a
horse screamed and went down and somebody cursed wildly
and Bratton heard a man hit the water at a run, heading at
a long angle toward the west shore a hundred feet away.
"Cover him," Bratton called, and fired his six-guns dry,
then loaded again as Kittle hammered his twin guns until
they popped empty. The rest of the posse joined in. The
running man was halfway across the river when he suddenly stopped as if he had hit a stone wall, then twisted
backward with a high, wild scream and fell heavily into
the water, floating facedown in a sluggish whirlpool.

"You . . . son . . , of . . . a . . . bitch . . . Timkins. . . ." a man screamed, and fired wildly as Bratton
called sharply between shots, "Save your ammo."

No more shots came from the west side of the river and
the next morning Bratton, still lying behind his rock,
looked around at the camp in the burgeoning light and
cursed silently. Red Heep lay across the coals dead, and
Bob Waters, a saloon keeper from town, sat ashen-faced, a
torn shirt bandage around his wounded leg. Bill Cane's
line-backed buckskin sprawled on its side, a great pool of
blood beneath it. Almost every cooking utensil around the
fire had been holed at least once.

Bratton, eyes fastened on the west bank of the river,
rose slowly. Other posse members stood up stiffly, and
one man moved Heep's body away from the coals and
covered him with a saddle blanket, muttering, "Now who
the hell's gonna tell his folks?"

Bratton looked out to the river where the dead posse
member floated. "Who's that out there?"

Cane looked up. "Harley Jones from the Bitterroot
Ranch."

"Somebody go get him outa there, all right?" Two
posse members walked to the edge of the river, then,

eyeing the opposite bank nervously, hesitated until Bratton ordered Cane and Kittle to cover them with rifles.

They ate a silent breakfast, then laid the two dead men out and covered them with stones to keep away the animals. Bratton, watching this unsavory task, thought bitterly, Two good boys gone and it's my damn fault. I underestimated this gent . . . and promised himself he'd never make that mistake again.

Half an hour later, they splashed up on the opposite bank, guns at the ready. Cane rode the dead Heep's horse and one of the other riders led Jones's mount.

Stopping beside Waters, Bratton said, "We're about fifteen miles north of Wickieup and the same distance from Kingman. You wanta try for Wickieup or Kingman?"

"Probably ain't no doc at Wickieup," Waters said. "Damned place always been a hideout for gunslicks and cow thieves. Best move on to Kingman."

"We got to get through the Hualapias," Bratton said. "They ain't much, but we could run up against 'Paches."

Waters looked straight at him, then said quietly, "If that happens, Del, maybe so we'll all wind up in hell," and rode on just as one of the posse members, a long-haired Mexican who had come along to track for Bratton, came back from a scout. "Señor," he said, "you should come and look," and turned his horse as Bratton grunted, "All right, Antonio. What ya got?"

Not answering, the Mexican led the sheriff to a backwater of the river and pointed to the center of a gray pool where a hat floated.

"Quicksand," Bratton breathed.

"Hell, that stuff ain't dangerous," Kittle said.

Waters rode up and looked bleakly at the floating hat. "Reckon that's old Rudy's hat, all right."

"Went under," another man said, and spit a stream of

tobacco juice at the gray surface, leaving an ugly smear on the deceptive sand.

Sitting there looking at the hat, Bratton was thinking how badly he had misjudged Timkins and because of that he turned to Antonio and said softly, "Make a circle. Keep it wide. Maybe half a mile out, then come back here."

"You figure he's foxing us?" asked Kittle, staring at the sheriff curiously. "Maybe you'd just like it more if he was pulling something on us so we could run the bastard down and hang him?"

"One way to find out," Bratton said reasonably, then pointed down river and said, "Cat, ride on down there for a mile or so. Look for tracks leaving the water. Carl, you cross over and ride downstream too just in case he rode south and then crossed over. A couple of you other fellers do the same upriver. We'll meet back here."

An hour later, Antonio returned and said, "He rode on the rocks, señor, then a mile out he went west toward Kingman."

Bratton raised one of his guns and fired three times, then waited.

"Señor." The Mexican spoke quietly and there was something in his voice that turned Bratton instantly alert. "Señor, I saw eight unshod horse tracks out there. They came from the north and they picked up Rudy's tracks . . . followed them. . . ."

Bratton sighed. " 'Paches," he said, and wondered why nothing ever seemed to go right.

"Sí, señor," Antonio agreed, and rolled a cigarette and passed the sack to Bratton.

Baldy Birch stepped off the Atchison, Topeka, and Sante Fe train at Albuquerque, saddle over his shoulder and Winchester dangling from his right hand. He walked easily along the loading platform, duly noting the two men wearing stars who lounged against the adobe wall of the station.

On a sudden impulse, the ex-sergeant walked over, nodded and asked, "Livery around here somewheres?"

One of the officers, a slim Mexican wearing a cross-draw holster and a shell belt with every loop filled, raised a delicate hand and pointed down street and said in excellent English, "One block south and one east."

Thanking him, Birch shifted the heavy stock saddle to a more comfortable position and strode along the platform and down the steps to the street.

Half an hour later, he rode south on a tough-looking bay gelding. Behind the saddle was strapped three days grub and in one saddlebag a bottle rested comfortably. Five miles from town, Birch pulled up the horse and unearthed the bottle, had a drink, and jogged on.

Three days later he rode into Kelly, New Mexico, and inquired at the livery stable as to where the Smackler spread was.

The hostler, a cool-eyed oldster who had seen his share of hardcases, carefully examined Birch, then said, "It's north of here and a little west, but they ain't nobody out there but the widder and the kid."

"Widder?" Birch asked.

"Yep, old Gene, he done robbed the bank, him and two other gents . . . fellers named Courtney and Jolly, and they wound up getting salivated over in Shakespeare, Arizona. Law caught up to 'em."

"Too bad," Birch said. "Always figgered that damn fool brother-in-law of mine would get hisself in trouble. Feller hated work too much. Guess I'll drift out and see how my sister's taking it."

When Birch rode up to Smackler's place, he found Molly sitting on the front porch. Pulling the horse in, he

hooked a leg around the horn and carefully rolled a cigarette as Molly watched, her eyes calm and unafraid.

"You're a long ways from Texas, Baldy," she observed.

Staring boldly at her full breasts, he grinned slowly and
said, "Looks like old Gene done run up against something
he just couldn't hack . . ."

"He's dead, if that's what you're saying," she told
him, and looked toward the barn just as her daughter came
out leading a pinto.

When the girl saw Baldy, she stopped for a moment,
then came on until she reached the steps. Looking curiously at the big man on the bay, she said, "Who's this
feller?"

Molly smiled. "Old friend of your paw's."

"He's a little late, ain't he, Maw?" the girl said. Staring at her, Birch realized she wasn't in the least disturbed
over the violent loss of her father. Like mother, like
daughter, he thought.

"Just a little," Molly agreed. "You going over to
Hameses' place now?"

Mounting swiftly, the girl smiled at Birch and said, "Be
nice to Mommy and she might invite you in for a cup of
coffee," and wheeled the little pinto and raced off toward
the west.

Birch looked at Molly for a long moment, then glanced
away when she refused to drop her eyes. "You came for a
reason," she finally said. "Why don't we just get at it and
never mind the talk?"

Birch jerked his head around and stared at her, then slid
off the bay, tied it to the porch and stepped up to her.
Taking a deep breath, he said, "After you, lady," and
watched as she rose and walked straight through the front
room to the bedroom, closing the door behind them.

Glancing at Birch, she said, "In case the girl comes
back for something," and began disrobing.

"Damn!" Birch exclaimed, and unbuckled his gunbelt and hung it over a bedpost.

Birch stayed that night and the next morning had breakfast with Molly and the girl, who had come home just before dark and, finding Birch still there, acted as if her mother entertained men every day. When she got up the next morning and discovered Birch's horse in the barn and the bedroom door still closed, she leaned an ear against the door and stood listening for a long time, her eyes wide and interested. After a while she bent and peeked through the keyhole as the sounds of lovemaking came clearly through the door. Now she sat eating, ignoring her mother and Birch, thinking, I'll probably have a brat brother to take care of now, and hating her mother and this big, powerful man.

When Birch rode out, Sissy watched him from the barn, then came to the house and, staring at her mother, asked "Why?"

Molly did not meet her daughter's eyes. Instead she continued to rock in the old chair she favored and kept her eyes on her knitting, but she said, "If I hadn't done that, he'd have taken me and probably you too."

"They'd hang him for sure," Sissy said reasonably.

"And just how would that help you?" Molly asked.

Sissy took a deep breath and said, "You're always warning me to stay out of the barn loft with Danny Hames because he'll cause me to have a baby, then you go and do the same thing right here in our house."

"I told you," Molly said sharply, "I was trying to keep that brute from raping us both. He would have, you know. I saw some of the things he did in Texas. He might have just hauled off and killed us both too."

The subject of Molly and Sissy's conversation was at that moment buying groceries in the Kelly Mercantile Store and whistling off-key through his teeth when a cold voice from the door said, "Turn around real slow, Birch, and if you so much as quiver, I'll make you part of the wall." Birch heard the twin clicks of a double-barreled shotgun being placed on full cock.

Turning his head carefully, he looked at the man standing in the doorway and then grinned in spite of the menacing bores of the heavy Greener pointed at his chest. "Low there, High Pockets. You kinda outa your bailiwick, now ain't ya?"

"I've got a warrant that says you're under arrest for murder and mayhem," the man said levelly.

Turning slowly, Birch looked the lawman over, noting the famous star of the Texas Rangers pinned to his left breast and the heavy .45 belted at his hip. Tied to a hitchrack directly behind him was a black horse covered with the dust and sweat of the trail.

"You figure you can get me back to Texas?" Birch asked, and it was as if he really wanted to know.

"I'll get you there," the lawman promised, and Birch shook his head and said softly, "Feller's too sure of himself," and fired from behind the sack of flour he held in front of him.

The bullet struck the ranger just below the bridge of his nose and angled upward, blasting away the top of his head and hurling it into the rafters. The shotgun sagged off at an angle, then went off with a thunderous roar as the ranger's trigger finger suddenly closed, sending both barrels straight into the grocer's stomach.

Smashed back against the wall, the man screamed, then bounced forward again to strike the counter, disappearing below its edge as blood fountained in great splashes over the floor.

Before the grocer hit the floor, the discharge of the shotgun jerked the already dead ranger off his feet, dropping him near the door.

Stepping over to the counter, Birch looked at the grocer and shook his head. "It's always the innocent bystander," he said as he lifted a .45 from a rack on the wall, punched out his empty round and quickly placed it in the .45, then dropped it near the grocer's right hand and went about gathering up the few groceries he needed.

By the time half a dozen townmen came cautiously through the door, Birch had filled his saddlebags, cleaned out the cash box and stuffed the roll of bills in a chap pocket, helped himself to a brand-new 38.40 Winchester rifle and a new .44 pistol. He looked at the curious faces peering in the door and said, "This here's one loco town. Me, I came in here and bought me some grub and a rifle and pistol and just got done paying for them when the grocer feller goes over to the wall and grabs a gun and shoots right past my shoulder. Me, I hit the floor and then that gent with the star cuts loose with the sawed-off and both these hombres is dead as a nit."

A man wearing a marshal's badge pushed through the crowd, growling, "Make way, there, men," and then stopped and looked at the dead ranger. "Damn, them forty-fives sure do make a hell of a mess at close range." Walking over to the counter, he looked at the dead grocer and added, "I reckon it's a toss-up which of them things does the most damage," and glanced at Birch. "Who're you?"

"Name's Hill Breech from Oklahoma country," Birch said. "Who're you?"

"Me, I'm Al Cooper, city marshal," and he pushed his hat to the back of his head. "What happened here?"

Birch repeated his story and then watched as Cooper went behind the counter and checked the .45, removed the spent round and said in wonder, "Damned fool only had one round in her."

"That was damn sure enough," a man wearing a barber's apron said.

Looking at Birch, Cooper asked, "That ranger say anything before this all happened?"

Birch pushed his hat back with the rifle barrel, "Yep, told the grocer he was under arrest for murder."

"Well, I'll be damned," one of the townsmen remarked, staring around at the others gathered there. "Who would have guessed the rangers was looking for old Ernie. Hell, I always figured if anybody was wanted by the law, it would be that there wife of his."

The sally was greeted by soft chuckles, which Cooper ignored, turning instead to a man dressed in black and wearing a bowler hat. "Thorpe, reckon you best get your wagon up here. These fellers is all yours now. I'll go tell the widder," and he went out, followed by Birch, who went to his horse and tied the bulging saddlebags to the cantleboard, lashed the stolen rifle on top of his yellow slicker and pushed the .44 beneath his shell belt.

"Thanks for the cooperation," Cooper said, and Birch nodded, waved and rode out of town, heading south.

"Tough-looking jasper," Cooper observed, and walked down street.

Rudy Timkins knew the Apaches were behind him. He had taken cover behind a low ridge and watched them dogtrotting their small desert horses along his back trail a mile behind him and wondered if he could beat them to Kingman and knew he was kidding himself.

"When they want me, they'll come get me," he told his horse, and lifted his canteen and drank deep.

Half an hour later, he swung around a high butte and worked his way to the top where a huge sentinel rock, its red sides glittering in the sun, thrust upward like some great finger pointing to heaven.

Dismounting, Timkins lifted his rifle from the scabbard, led the horse around to the shady side of the rock and stood looking toward his back trail. Far off across the great jagged reaches of the Hualapia Mountains he could see the tip of Hualapia Peak reaching better than eight thousand feet above sea level. From where he stood the desert extended for several miles east, cut across here and there by jagged cross-canyons. It was a desolate stretch of country.

Far out toward the distant mountains he could just make out cloud of dust being kicked up by several riders and thought, The damn posse . . . then looked closer to his own location and saw two horsemen riding straight toward him and two more circling wide to the north. He knew there was probably two or three more riding in a loop around to the south of his position and thought bleakly, I reckon this here's where I make my stand, and wondered if the posse would reach him before the Indians got him.

"Sure don't make a hell of a lot of difference," he told himself. "Injuns'll scalp me and the posse, they'll stretch my neck . . . some damn choice."

Going to his horse, he dug into the saddlebags and pulled out a box of rifle shells and an extra shell belt, its loops filled with .45 rounds. He tied the animal to a jutting piece of stone farther beneath the overhang of rock that shaded him, and slinging the extra shell belt over his shoulders, dumped the rifle rounds in his pockets. Moving carefully around the edge of the rock tower, for he knew the Apaches had to be getting close, he slid in among a pile of boulders just as he heard a falling rock rattle down the slope in front of his position.

Lifting his head very carefully after removing his hat, he found himself staring at two Indians sitting their horses less than fifty feet away. Very slowly he laid the notched back sight on the Apache facing him and shot him through the body, immediately jacking another round into the chamber and firing at the second Indian just as he dived from his horse in a sprawling attempt to escape the first man's fate.

The Indian was a second late. Timkins' slug struck him in the back, breaking the spinal column and killing him instantly.

Turning then, he looked south and watched four mounted riders break from cover and come headlong up the slope as the sound of scrambling horses came to him from the north side of the pinnacle. Trying to ignore the danger from behind, he lifted the rifle, sighted it carefully and shot one of the riders from the saddle. As the man's body struck the ground and bounced in among a scattering of boulders, the other three Apaches suddenly swerved their mounts away and seemingly vanished into thin air.

Turning then, he stepped around the rock looking for the warriors he knew must be almost on top of his position and was in time to see them disappear below him in the rocks.

Wondering what had made them cut away, he hurried back to his former position and then chuckled. Below him, riding full tilt with guide-ons snapping in the breeze and sabers flashing in the sun, was a troop of cavalry, their blue coats and the officers' long capes distinctive against the brown of the desert.

He calmly mounted his horse, and rode down slope, meeting the troop at the base of the pinnacle. A tall officer galloped forward, saluted, and Timkins, out of old habit, almost saluted in return, but then caught himself and said, "In the nick of time, huh, Captain?"

The officer smiled. "Looked like you was in for a fight of it," and he glanced to where his men were searching the rocks for the Apaches. "Waste of time. Never catch them 'Paches now."

"Which way you heading, Captain?" Timkins asked.

"We're on our way back to Kingman. Give you an escort, sir?"

Timkins glanced back to where the soldiers were riding cautiously among the boulders, carbines at the ready, and nodded. "Sure would appreciate it, Captain. I don't hanker for them Apaches to get a second run at me."

They arrived at Kingman late that evening and Timkins thanked the captain then went in search of a livery, where he sold his horse, an animal he had stolen when he broke jail. Calmly writing out a bill of sale, he told the liveryman, "That there's a damn good horse. I've had him since he was born. Handles like he was part human and sits like Grandma's old rocking chair."

Heaving his saddle and gear on his back and carrying the rifle he had stolen on the way out of the Prescott jail, he walked to the Wells Fargo office and dropping his gear in a corner, asked the stationmaster, "When's the next stage leave for Tombstone?"

The stationmaster, a high-shouldered man who walked as if his boots were too tight and his gunbelt was pinching his waist, scratched his head. "Be in here at midnight and will leave half an hour later. You want a ticket, get it now and don't show up drunk or old Jake Salsbury, he's the driver, he won't let you aboard. Religious man, he is. Don't cotton to drunks, owlhoots, loose women or drummers."

Timkins bought a ticket, then, thinking about the posse that even now could be riding into town, said, "I've got a friend out on the edge of town lives beside the Tombstone road. I'll catch the stage there. Reckon you can tell this Salsbury I'll be waiting?"

"He'll stop, if he don't take you for a road agent and fill you full of buckshot," the stationmaster said dispassionately.

Timkins retrieved his gear and left the station, immediately walking west a block, then following a rough side street to the southern edge of town, where he cut back east again, sat down behind a large rock and promptly dozed off.

When Watson and Vent arrived back at the hotel, they found a large crowd gathered around the bodies sprawled in the dining room. Carpenter was just rising from an examination of Smackler. Seeing Vent, he turned and, glancing at Watson, asked, "Mind telling me what this was all about?"

"Have you talked to Deputy Putnam?" Vent countered.

"I talked to him," Carpenter said. "Told him he was damn well out of his bailiwick and had no call to go shooting up my town."

Vent shook his head. "These old boys didn't give us no other way to go," he pointed out as the Preacher came over, followed closely by Joe Helger.

Helger looked at Carpenter and then back at Watson. "Preacher, here, says these gents hit the bank at Kelly. Lit out with over fifty thousand dollars," and the naked greed in the deputy's eyes was plain to see.

Nodding to where Angel Brown sat in a chair sipping a glass of water an attentive clerk had fetched her, Vent said, "Money belongs to Miss Brown's father. He's the banker. His daughter came along to take it back if we caught up with these fellers."

While the two local lawmen talked to Vent, he had noticed Putnam quietly climbing the stairs, and now he came back down carrying two bulging saddlebags.

"Looks like Smackler and his boys didn't have much chance to spend the money," he said, hefting the full bags.

Carpenter looked down at them and then said, "I'll have to take possession of that money until you folks can prove it really belongs to Miss Brown and her daddy."

The Preacher grinned frostily. Watson dropped his hand to one of his guns and Vent looked coldly at the marshal and said, "No, I don't think so. I think maybe we'll just sorta hang on to this money ourselves. Like to see it get back to the Kelly bank. Folks back there need it."

Helger, whose face was slowly turning crimson, snapped, "Look, me and Rand here are the law in Shakespeare. What we say goes. If Rand says we take the money, then by God we take the money," and he started to reach for the bags.

"Touch those bags and I'll send you to hold old Smackler's hand, wherever he is," the Preacher said coldly, a wolfish grin plastered on his face.

Looking at him, Helger stepped back. "Hey, you threatening me, old man?"

"Mr. Helger, you are getting damn tiresome," the Preacher observed. "Now if you don't break this off, I'm going to punch your ticket, and if that thing there calling itself a marshal reaches for his gun, the undertaker's going to have a damn full day tomorrow."

Rand turned and said, "Let it be, Joe," then looking at Vent, he asked: "They was a third feller. He get away?"

"He made it as far as an alley south of here. You'll find him there." Vent looked down at his injured leg and saw the rip in his pants and the smear of blood and asked, "Sawbones around here?"

Helger, whose face was even redder now, was not going to let it lie, Vent knew, and he waited for what must come. Helger did not disappoint him.

"I ain't gonna take no crap from a old has-been," he snapped, glaring at the Preacher.

Carpenter, who was obviously much smarter than the deputy, said, "Leave it be, Joe. You mess with the Preacher, he'll weight you down with lead and the county will just have to dig up another man."

Pointing a trembling finger at the Preacher, Helger snarled, "If these fellers shoots one of us, the whole damn town will string 'em up."

Staring at him, Carpenter said disgustedly, "Hell of a lot of good that'll do us."

A sizable crowd had gathered, and now a small man wearing black gamblers' garb and two six-shooters partially concealed beneath the tails of a long morning coat stepped through a suddenly respectful crowd and pushed his flat-crowned black hat to the back of a head covered with curly blond hair. "Rand, you and Joe wouldn't be trying a little highbinding, now would you?"

Looking around, Helger said sullenly, "You stay outa this, Gil Monroe."

Vent, upon hearing the name, looked keenly at the diminutive gambler. He had heard of him through half a dozen mining camps. Monroe was one of those oddities among the card fraternity, an honest gambler. Some said he didn't need to cheat because he carried the devil's own luck around with him. He was also as fast as snapping chain lightning with handgun or knife.

Apparently the Preacher knew him as well, for he glanced at him and said, "Long time, Gil."

The gambler smiled and the light from a dangling lamp struck quick fire from a gleaming set of perfect teeth. "That it has been," and nodding at Vent, said, "Leatherhand, welcome to hell."

Vent smiled faintly and Watson, who had been sizing up Monroe, decided he was in their corner and turned to Carpenter. "Marshal, they just ain't no way we're going to turn over this money to you or Mr. Helger. That's final. You best go away and sleep on it."

Helger snarled, "By God, we take that money in our protection without violence or we take it at gunpoint. Now which will you have?"

The room was suddenly silent. Helger, even though he was a fool, had laid down a challenge and Vent knew one of them must take it up. He had about decided to kill the idiot when Monroe laughed, breaking the silence. Others took it up and Monroe walked over to Helger and slapped him on the back. "Boy, Joe, you sure as hell got a lot of hard bark on you. Here you are, challenging two of the fastest men to ever strap on a forty-five and you ain't even nervous."

Helger, taken aback, suddenly tried on a grin, then shook his head. "Reckon I must be crazy." As Carpenter stared at him in amazement, he turned and walked out, remarking to no one in particular, "Me, I'm gonna get me a drink."

"You know, I've worked with that feller for two years," the marshal said, "and I sure as hell ain't figured out his pedigree yet."

"Acts like he's as crazy as a mad woman slinging crap on a mountainside," observed the Preacher.

Angel came over then and said, "Mr. Putnam, the clerk told me we can take stage to Las Cruces, then make a connection that will carry us to Kelly if we're at the depot in half an hour."

An hour later the stage was ready to roll out of town. Aboard it was Angel Brown and Putnam, their horses tied to the rear of the coach and their saddles stacked on top.

As she was about to board, Angel turned and walked to Vent. "If you ever get tired of traipsing around the country shooting folks, why not come back to Kelly? Who knows, I might still be single." Then she smiled archly, kissed him lightly on the cheek and stepped aboard.

Putnam, riding shotgun beside the driver, lifted a proprietary boot and planted it on top of the Wells Fargo strongbox wherein lay the Kelly bank's money and observed to no one in particular, "Some fellers have all the blamed luck."

Monroe, leaning against the side of the depot, watched the stage leave, then invited Vent and his two companions down street for a drink. Pushing through the swinging doors of the Dry Hole Saloon where Monroe ran a faro game and an occasional poker layout, they took a table near the back and sat until the bartender brought over drinks.

Rand Carpenter and Joe Helger leaned against the bar near the back door, and Vent, watching them, had an odd feeling as if something was about to happen. He saw the Preacher move uneasily, then lift his coattails clear of his guns and slip off the leather tiedowns. Taking his cue from the Preacher, Vent removed the hammer tiedown from his .44 and watched the two lawmen narrowly.

Monroe hadn't missed these moves. He turned and peered sharply toward the lawmen, then let his eyes travel up the stairs while Vent watched him, wondering if he too felt the strain in the air.

Deciding to find out, he lifted his drink and said from behind it, "Things seem a little tense in here. . . . Any idea why?"

"None." Monroe shook his head slightly, but added, "I got that old feeling. . . ."

The Preacher carefully examined each customer, as did Watson.

"Anything?" Vent asked.

"Nothing," the Preacher said.

"It's here," Monroe insisted.

"You got any problems, Gil?" the Preacher asked, his eyes still roaming the room.

"None that I know of, but hell, Preacher, you know this business. Kill a feller in Deadwood and a year later his brother tries to gun you in the back in Dallas."

Looking around again, Vent suddenly realized the usual sounds of a saloon operating full bore were absent. Not only were the men scattered around the room not talking, but the women, who were usually laughing shrilly or teasing some cowboy, were silent, their eyes going everywhere but in the direction of Vent's table.

"Where's the piano player?" the Preacher asked casually.

"Damned if I know," Monroe said. "Hell, he should be sitting up there ahammering away."

The bartender turned halfway to his left and Vent saw his eyes widen, and then Vent rose and drew and fired into a curtain at the end of the bar, saw his bullet fan the cloth to one side and chunk solidly into a body.

On the instant of Vent's move, Monroe and the Preacher had drawn swiftly, as had Watson, and now they stood in a semicircle around the table, their guns neatly bracketing the room.

As all eyes locked into the curtain, someone coughed behind it, then a man wearing a sombrero and crossed shell belts toppled into the room, dragging the curtain with him. His fist gripped an unfired pistol, and when he hit the floor, he did not move.

A sigh went around the room, then the bartender walked down the bar and gingerly leaned over the body. "This here greaser, he's dead as last week's tortillas."

No one moved. Glancing at Monroe, Vent suggested, "Maybe you can put a name on him," and watched as the gambler, gun dangling at the end of his arm, walked over. Shaking his head, Monroe said, "He don't read nothing to me. Looks like a border jumper."

Carpenter and Helger, who hadn't moved during the shooting, now went to the body and, using his toe, Carpenter rolled the dead man over, grimaced as he noted the gaping hole just over the man's heart, and said, "Hell, this here's Jesus Vigary. He's a hardcase that works for the Diamond-D Silver and Cattle Company outa Tombstone."

The Preacher holstered his pistol and lifted his drink. "Know who owns that lashup?" he asked casually.

"Sure," a miner drinking alone at a table said. "Everybody has heard of the Diamond-D. Belongs to Colonel Bill Alex. Big war hero, so they say."

Watson stared at the man. "Feller must have been drunk or he was after you, Mr. Monroe."

"Well, it's a certain cinch he was after somebody at that table," Carpenter growled.

"Looked to me like he was pointing that gun at Mr. Watson," Helger said.

"Oh?" Watson turned then, and added, "How come you didn't try and stop him?"

Helger grinned. "Hell, I figured he'd punch your ticket. Me, I just damn don't like you, so I figured why take a chance on gettin' plugged trying to save your hide."

Monroe grinned. "Now that makes more sense than anything I've heard all day."

The Preacher grinned his wolfish grin and observed, "Well, at least he tells her the way she lays."

"It might get him salivated some day too," Watson said and turned to Vent. "Me. I'm going to bed. This here town's just too damn tough for me," and he holstered his gun and walked out.

Nodding after him, Vent said, "Better trail along, Preacher," and watched as the tall old gambler moved out on soundless feet.

Monroe looked at Vent and then asked curiously, "He still as good as he usta be?"

"I didn't know him when he was marshaling, but I know I'd think a long time before going to the gun with him," Vent answered.

Carpenter said, "Mr. Torrey, I reckon you and your friends had better stay around until we can have a coroner's inquest. Any objections?"

"How long will it take?" Vent asked.

Carpenter grinned. "Ask Mr. Monroe. He's the coroner."

"First thing in the morning," Monroe said. "I'll meet you for breakfast at the hotel."

At nine a.m. Vent rode out of Shakespeare, trailed by Watson and the Preacher. Ahead was a long, hot ride to Tombstone, behind them a coroner's verdict absolving them of all blame for the shootings.

As they mounted in front of the livery, Monroe had come along the street and said, "Nice doing business with you fellers . . . I also own the undertaking parlor."

"They anything in this here shebang you don't own?" Watson asked.

Monroe thought a moment, then said, "I don't own the meat market or the boot shop and several of the mines belong to other folks."

"What about the law?" Vent asked, and watched Monroe's eyes.

They showed nothing and Vent decided the man had earned his reputation for being a good poker player. Now Monroe shrugged and said, "As much as you can own any man," and stepped back and smiled faintly as Vent turned his horse and rode away.

Chapter 5

A desert wind was pushing the tumbleweeds along the banks of washouts when Vent, the Preacher and Watson rounded into Allen Street on tired horses at four o'clock in the afternoon. It was a time when the denizens of Tombstone's nightlife were just stirring about and the businessmen were beginning to look forward to their evening drink with anticipation. Although the saloons were open, there was very little business at this time of day.

As Vent's party rode along the wide, unpaved street, its dirt hard-packed by a driving sun and a sea of horses' hooves, everything appeared serene, belying the reputation of this wild, silver boom town, where grudges were settled with guns and knives. It was no place for the lilly-livered or weak-kneed, Vent knew.

When the day turned to night and the coal-oil lamps were lit, this sprawling collection of board-and-bat shacks and thick-walled adobes turned into a raging hell, punctuated by the roar of guns and the bellow of men on the prod, whose capacity for liquor was only exceeded by their penchant for violence.

As Vent led the Preacher and Watson across Sixth Street, a slim, blond dandy in a neat gray suit strolled from the Oriental Saloon and placed a shoulder against a porch support, his hat slightly slanted over his eyes.

"Tinhorn," Watson observed, staring at the man.

"Probably," Vent agreed, a faint smile on his face.

"They say this here town's got a lot of meat-eaters in it," Watson said. "If that's an example, I ain't worried."

On the outskirts of town a sign tacked to a post had informed them that guns were off limits in Tombstone and had to be checked at the police station or Cochise County courthouse. Vent had slipped the .44 behind his belt, making certain his coattails covered its telltale bulk, then thrust the shellbelt and holster into a saddlebag.

"I advise you boys to do the same," he counseled. The Preacher was already in the process of removing his twin .45s. He shoved them under his belt with the butts forward. Vent, seeing this, grinned and remarked, "You figure on becoming a Wild Bill follower?"

The Preacher looked sour. "That feller, and they's them that'll argue whether he is a feller or not, built his rep on back shooting and drunk killing."

"Hell, he's pretty damn fast," Watson protested.

"Get enough practice on still targets and you're bound to get good," the Preacher grunted, and looked pointedly at Watson's guns. "You better shuck them irons."

"To hell with this town and its gun laws," Watson said roughly, and started to ride on.

Shrugging, the Preacher looked at Vent. "Hate to lose a relative, seeing as how I ain't got that many, but then it's your choice . . . you want your remains shipped back to Texas or planted here?"

Watson pulled his horse in and stared at the old gambler.

"Now who the hell's gonna do for me?" he asked.

"Well, you can kinda take your choice," Vent said.

"There's Virgil Earp, the marshal, and then there's Wyatt Earp; I think he's a U.S. marshal or something. Oh, yeah, and Johnny Behan, he's the sheriff. He just naturally don't cotton to strangers. Kinda figures they may be hired guns trying to cut his herd, seeing as he controls most of the funny business around here."

"Funny business?" Watson asked.

"Yep, you know, like stagecoach robbing, stealing cattle and such like . . ."

In the end Watson removed his guns and hid one in his inside coat pocket and the other behind his belt and they rode on.

Now Vent turned his horse and rode to the edge of the sidewalk and nodded at the man in the gray suit. " 'Lo, Doc. How's things with you?"

"Fine as frog's hair," the man answered in a soft southern drawl. "Been quite a little spell since you and me crossed trails . . . last time was Dodge, wasn't it?"

"Yep, had a little trouble there, if I recall. Seems as how you sorta sidled in and give me a hand."

"Heard you put a bunch of fellers down before that game was done," the man said.

"Me and the Preacher here, and a couple of other good men," Vent agreed.

The man in gray nodded at the Preacher, smiled and said, "Howdy, Preacher. Ain't you ever gonna die?"

"By and by, Holliday. Every man to his time."

"Ummm . . . you'll outlive me, that's a certainty."

Vent jerked his head toward Watson and said, "This here's Jim Watson, Preacher's nephew from Texas. Owns a spread up there. Jim, meet Doc Holliday."

Watson smiled thinly and said, "My pleasure, Mr. Holliday. May we buy you a drink?"

"Why thank you, Mr. Watson, but this here's my town. I'll buy the first round." Then he turned his gaze down

street and watched three men trotting their horses toward
Fourth Street and the half smile disappeared as if it had
never been and his eyes frosted over as he made a slight
half turn and hooked his thumbs in a heavy shell belt.

"Friends of yours?" Vent asked.

Holliday glanced at Vent, then answered softly, "You
might say I know them. Run a spread west of Charleston.
That's Ike, Phineas and Billy Clanton. Nice fellers . . ."

Vent noticed they were not carrying guns and wondered
how Holliday got away with wearing his, then thought
ruefully, who was going to brace him and take them
away? "Livery around close?" he asked.

Holliday nodded down street and said, "OK Corral a
block west on Fremont. About as good a place as you'll
find in Tombstone . . . 'sides, it's far enough away from
Allen and Tough-Nut streets to eliminate the possibility of
one of the horses getting plugged by some damn fool
shooting off his pistol."

"We'll put the animals away and come back for that
drink," Vent said. "You prefer any particular place?"

"Well, since my friend Mr. Earp owns a piece of the
Oriental, I guess I'd best patronize him," he said, and
nodded as the Clantons turned off Allen Street and rode
out of sight toward Fremont.

Vent led the way over onto Fremont, watching the
Clantons turn into the hitchrack in front of a building with
a large sign that said this was Bauer's Meat Market.

As Vent's party jogged past, one of the men looked up,
scowled and acted as if he were about to say something,
but then his brother placed a restraining hand on his arm
and they turned and tramped inside.

Walking back toward Allen Street, where the night people were just starting to appear, Vent saw a town like so
many of the gold-rush camps he had marshaled. The only
difference here was one of metals. Silver had built Tomb-

stone and before its glory faded it would produce twenty-five million dollars' worth of ore and fill a large cemetery with its victims.

There were horses lining the hitchracks now and men fanned the saloon doors as they walked or staggered from place to place. The high tinkle of rinky-dink pianos pushed their sounds into the street where whores walked arm in arm with miners, gamblers and cowboys in off the range, loaded for a night on the town. Before morning they would be broke and ready for another month of chasing longhorns out of the thornbrush along the San Pedro River. As they approached the Oriental on the corner of Fifth and Allen streets, a tall man wearing a black hat and black suit came along the sidewalk from the direction of Sixth Street, paused to allow room for two men to roll into the dust in locked combat and then turned into the Oriental. Vent recognized Wyatt Earp and glanced at the Preacher, who said mildly, "Mr. Earp is beginning to show a bit of wear."

"He's lived a hard life." Vent chuckled.

They followed him into a long room crowded with men around faro tables and seated at poker layouts, each man with his small stack of chips and his eyes greedily fastened on the falling cards. At the far end of the room, a Negro played a piano. Along the bar the occasional bright splash of a soiled dove's dress clashed brutally with the harsh garb worn by the miners and cowboys.

"There's Doc," the Preacher said, nodding toward a table in the back of the room where the famed gunfighter sat with Earp and another man, who resembled Earp. Vent figured he must be one of the famous lawman's brothers.

As they made their way toward the table, several of the gamblers glanced at the Preacher and, apparently recognizing him, nodded, then spoke to their friends, who in turn looked up, took the Preacher's inventory and returned to concentrating on losing their money.

A man near the back of the room watched Vent's approach, his eyes cold and distant. To the Missourian, the man looked familiar. He was almost to Holliday's table when a chair slammed over and the watcher lunged to his feet and reached beneath his coat, shouting, "Torrey, you bastard, you killed my brother," and drew a six-shooter.

Men dived for cover, including Holliday and Earp, as Vent made a swift half turn, drew his gun from beneath his coat and fired in one smooth, controlled motion that was so fast the men who witnessed it were to say later it was a magical thing.

His bullet struck the gunman in the center of the chest, driving him backward against a mirror that shattered on impact. As he collapsed against it, glass skittered along the bar and the dying gunny choked out, "Oh, Jesus, Oh Jesus . . . He's did . . . for . . . me . . . Ohhhhh," and fell sideways, burying his dead face in the sawdust of the bar-room floor.

Gun still in hand, Vent cat-walked to where the man lay, knelt and had his look, then, walking over to Holliday's table, punched out the empty and replaced it with a shell from his pocket.

Holliday, Wyatt and the third man rose, and it was then Vent saw the badge on that one's shirt pocket and guessed this was probably Morgan Earp, an assistant marshal of Tombstone.

"Mr. Torrey, I'd be pleased if you would surrender your weapon and accompany me to the city hall," Morgan said.

Vent glanced at Holliday, who said mildly, "We'll come along, Mr. Torrey, and see if we can't convince the judge to allow you your freedom on your own recognizance."

Vent handed his gun to the marshal. "You'll be Morgan, that right?"

"I'm Morgan Earp, Mr. Torrey," the youngest of the Earp clan said.

As Vent handed over his gun, he felt suddenly naked. "Mr. Earp, you are the first man I ever surrendered my gun to. My life now lies in your hands."

"We'll take the best of care of it," Morgan promised, and led the way from the saloon, leaving the house to arrange for the removal of the dead man.

As they tramped along Allen Street, a short, stocky man hurried up to Earp. "What's going on here, Wyatt?"

"Evening, Mr. Clum," Holliday said. "Nothing much. Feller down at the Oriental pulled a gun on this young man and now he's riding a cloud. We're going along to city hall and see if the judge won't release him on his own word."

Clum looked at Vent, then, noticing his gloved right hand, said with some astonishment, "What the devil's Leatherhand doing in Tombstone?"

"Him, oh, he just dropped by to visit me," Holliday said. "We're old friends. First met Mr. Torrey in Kansas. We been kinda running into each other ever since."

"Who'd he kill?" Clum asked.

"Vent, this nosy gent is John P. Clum. Runs the *Tombstone Epitaph* newspaper. Looks like he wants to let folks know you're in town."

Vent looked at the former Indian agent and smiled. "Mr. Clum, I've heard of you and the work you did with the Indians. They say you were one of the best agents the government ever assigned out here. You have my respect, sir, but if you put my name before the people of this town, I'll spend most of my time taking this here walk over to the judge's office posting bail."

"Oh, how so?" Clum asked, taking two steps to Earps one as they rounded onto Fremont.

"I've made a few enemies along the way, and like that gent who just pulled on me at the Oriental, they's some who just gotta make a try," Vent explained.

"That feller you plugged was named Cody," Holliday said. "Seems he had a brother up around Jerome that just sorta got in the way of one of your slugs."

"Been around town long?" Vent asked.

"Rode in two days ago," Earp said as they pushed through the door of city hall and trudged back to the judge's chambers, where they found that worthy sitting by a window reading a heavy law book by the light of a candle.

"Pretty hard on your eyes, reading like that, Judge," Morgan observed.

Glancing up, the judge said sourly, "Danged cheap city council won't pay for coal oil. Figure I should pay for it out of my fines."

"Got a little business for you," Morgan said.

The judge rose, shrugged into a long black coat, mounted the bench, picked up a gavel and, hitting a block of wood once, said, "Magistrate's court of Tombstone, Arizona, Cochise County, now in session. What's before the bench?"

Morgan nodded his head toward Vent. "This here feller, Mr. Vent Torrey . . ." and the judge held up his hand and asked, "Did you say Torrey?"

Morgan nodded. "Yes sir, I said Torrey."

"Vent Torrey, the man called Leatherhand?" the judge asked.

"Yep, this here's the man."

"Who'd he plug?"

Vent smiled and the Preacher looked away, but some of the frost in his eyes melted. Glancing at him, the judge said, "What brings you to Tombstone, Preacher?"

"Cards," the Preacher said.

"Figures," the judge grunted.

"Mr. Torrey here came into the Oriental peaceable like at the invite of Mr. Holliday. As Mr. Torrey and his friends had just arrived in our town, Mr. Holliday thought it neighborly to ask them to join him in a drink. . . ."

"Birds of a feather," the judge observed.

"Yes sir," Morgan agreed, smiling faintly. "Well, when Mr. Torrey here come waltzing through the door, a gent by the name of Cody pops up and bellers out that Leatherhand here done for his brother and by God he was going to even her up."

"Let me guess the rest." The judge held up his hand. "The damn fool went for his gun and Mr. Torrey just naturally shot him dead. Is that correct?"

"That's about the size of it," Morgan said.

"Looks like a pure case of self-defense," the judge noted. "Any witnesses?"

Nodding at Wyatt, Morgan said, "Well, brother Wyatt here was present, as was the Preacher and his friend," and he glanced at Watson, whom he hadn't as yet met.

"This here's Jim Watson," Holliday said. "Rancher from Texas."

"Friend of yours?" the judge asked Vent.

"Yes sir, he's with us," Vent answered.

"Ummm . . . Well, Wyatt, do you agree with your brother's testimony?"

"I do," Wyatt said.

"I agree. That's the way it happened," Watson said.

"What about you, Preacher? You agree?"

The Preacher nodded and the judge said, "Let the record show the witness answered in the affirmative . . . by the way, Preacher, you got any other name?"

"Useta have, but it got lost along the way somewhere," the Preacher said.

"I'll just bet it did." The judge grinned. "How came this hombre to try for you, Mr. Torrey?"

"Killed his brother up in the Val Verde Valley some years back," Vent admitted.

"You seem to have a knack for getting into feuds, don't you, Mr. Torrey?"

Vent met the judge's eyes and held them until the judge finally coughed and looked away, then said, "Sorry about that, Mr. Torrey. Not in this court's purview . . . I'm going to rule justifiable homicide in this case, but I'm also going to fine you twenty-five dollars for carrying a pistol inside the city limits. You got the money?"

Vent dug out two ten-dollar gold pieces and five silver dollars and handed them over and the judge, who said, "Bring that candle over here so I can enter this in the books." When Morgan complied, he laboriously scrawled the amount of the fine, what it was for and Vent's name in a large journal. "That's all, gentlemen, court's adjourned," and as they turned and started to leave the room, the judge cleared his throat and said, "Mr. Torrey, if your victim lacks relatives here to bury him or he's broke, then you'll be required to do so. City can't afford it, or at least that's what they claim."

"I'll do that," Vent said, and followed Earp and Holliday through the door and out onto Fremont Street, where they found the Clantons sitting on the steps of the meat market across the way watching them.

"Now we go get that drink," Holliday said, as Clum nodded and walked away.

When they reentered the Oriental, the body was gone and the only indication a man had died was the empty mirror frame and new sawdust on the floor beneath it. Walking to a table near the rear of the room, Holliday sat with his back to the wall and Morgan and Wyatt ranged alongside him, leaving Vent, the Preacher and Watson with their backs to the door.

Looking levelly at Morgan, Vent said, "Mr. Morgan, as

I've paid a fine for carrying a gun seems as how I should now be allowed to do so.''

Morgan looked around at Wyatt and shook his head. ''This feller missed his calling. He should have been a lawyer,'' but he slipped the gun from beneath his gunbelt and handed it to Vent, who tucked it back behind his coattails again and suddenly, with the .44 back in place, felt a swift surge of relief. The others around the table seemed to understand exactly what he was feeling.

''Trouble with a man who lives his life sleeping with a gun instead of a woman, he gets so he can't be without it,'' Holliday observed.

''Not much different with a woman. Same thing happens,'' Wyatt said.

A waiter came over, nervously accepted their order, then hurried back with a bottle of whiskey and glasses. Each man took a glass and filled it and Doc said, ''Here's to a man's need for a woman and a good horse. May he always have both beneath him when they are required.''

Smiling faintly, the Preacher downed his drink and, as each man followed suit, reached for the bottle again, filled his glass and leaned back, letting the amber fluid sit before him as he carefully inventoried the room. Vent had his careful look too, noting half a dozen punchers lining the bar. Sprinkled among them were women wearing off-the-shoulder dresses, their faces maps of the hard life they lived. Leaning nonchalantly at the far end of the bar, a huge man who Vent had pegged earlier as the bouncer stared at himself in the back-bar mirror. Such an individual working in Tombstone must walk a pretty tight line, Vent figured, what with half the gunfighters in the West drifting in and out. The bouncer could probably break a man's neck with one twist of his powerful hands, but when it came to shucking a gun, Vent would bet he was as slow as the mail. More than likely he's careful who he tosses out of here, Vent guessed.

The Preacher and Vent made their inventories, looking for old enemies and the possibility of new ones. Vent knew the Preacher was doing so. They both knew they could never ride into a strange town and go about their business as other men could. To do so might invite a bullet in the back.

"Know that gent in the suit at the far end of the bar by the window?" Vent asked the Preacher.

"That's Colonel William J. Alex, owner of the Diamond-D Silver and Cattle Company," Wyatt volunteered.

Watson turned slowly, met the man's eyes and looked away. Vent, watching the move, could have sworn something passed between the two.

He wondered if the Preacher had caught it, then decided he was probably letting his imagination get a choke hold on him and went back to his whiskey. But he was surprised when he saw the Preacher's eyes on the man by the window and wondered if his first evaluation had been accurate. He had learned never to underrate the Preacher's astuteness.

The man at the window table tossed off the remainder of his drink, and, when the bartender held up a bottle, shook his head, rose and strolled out the door, stepping to one side to allow two drunken cowboys entrance.

The big man at the end of the bar moved down the room and intercepted the loud-talking drunks. Grasping each by the shoulder with a powerful hand, the big man said mildly, "Now, me bys, ye know oi've told ye not to come in this place in yer present condition. Look at ye. Yer're a shameless sight. What would yer sainted mithers think if they could se ye now?"

One of the cowboys rolled owl eyes at the bouncer and

said, "Hey now, lesh keep me mither . . . my mother, to hell outa this here powwow."

The other rider jerked his shoulder away and snarled, "This mick's looking for a fat lip, Jody. Le's jus' give it to him," and suiting action to words, swung a wild roundhouse, which the bouncer neatly avoided and, grinning gleefully, reached out his long arms. Grasping each man by the outside of his head, he slammed them together loud enough to almost drown out the piano. Watson flinched and said, "Damn, but that musta hurt."

Holliday grinned. "I doubt if they even felt it," he said, and watched as the Irishman picked up the limp bodies of his victims and, carrying them to the door, heaved them into the street, brushed off his hands and returned to the end of the bar, slapping one of the soiled doves on the rear as he passed. She ignored him.

"How's the games going?" the Preacher asked Holliday.

"Not bad. Lot of silver money around. Rustlers been stealing cattle down in Mexico and pushing them back up here. Sell them to the army out at Fort Hauchuca. Army uses the meat—what they don't steal—to feed the Apaches over at San Carlos."

"Apaches giving you much of a problem?" Watson asked.

Earp nodded. "It's worth a man's life to fool around the Dragoons. That's the stomping grounds of the Chircahuas. Their leader, Vitorio, he just don't cotton to white folks."

Suddenly Holliday bent over the table in a coughing fit, dabbing his handkerchief at his mouth as the paroxysm slowly subsided. When he straightened up again, his face was white and the handkerchief was spotted with blood.

Vent stared at this quiet, blond-haired man with death eating at his lungs and wondered how long he would live. No man with his disease could long survive life in a smoke-filled room with whiskey for medicine and one meal a day. Yet somehow, the thin gunman had outlived all bets and, although Vent had no way of knowing, would linger on several more years before he died with his boots off, beating even longer odds than those generated by his diseased lungs.

Wyatt Earp, whose blond hair, blue eyes and rail-thin six-foot frame could have passed him off as Holliday's brother, ignored the dentist's coughing, poured the dentist's glass full again and waited until he gulped it down to tip the jug yet a third time. Vent had heard of the deadly doctor's capacity for liquor and wondered where he put it. No one had ever seen Doc Holliday drunk. If an enemy had caught him in that condition, he probably wouldn't be sitting there across from Vent gulping whiskey. Vent had long ago learned that men in his profession either learned to handle their whiskey or went to an early grave.

"Army bring much of that cattle money to town?" the Preacher asked, ignoring Holliday in his turn, out of politeness.

"Quite a bit, but they give Virgil and Morgan here a hard way to go sometimes," Wyatt said.

"They dearly love to fight," Morgan grunted, looking sourly at three uniformed men leaning on the bar, each with a drink in front of him.

"They gamble?" the Preacher wanted to know.

"Yep, they gamble," Holliday said. "Damn fools are always trying to cheat. Most of 'em come from the South, and someone must have once told all southerners they were born card thieves. I've had a run-in with a couple of them for messing with the discards and trying to second-card me."

A brief altercation erupted at the bar when one man threw whiskey in another's face and the two began swinging wildly at each other. Vent watched as the big bouncer, moving amazingly fast for one of his bulk, grabbed each of the fighters by the collar, dragged them to the door and hurled them into the street, where a crowd quickly gathered as they continued their disagreement.

"That bouncer's a pretty fair hand," Watson said.

A thin man came over and said quietly, "Pete Spence just came in the back, Doc. He's there in a game," and he nodded toward a door that now stood open. Vent looked that way and saw several men seated around a poker table, playing cards.

Holliday stood up. "Gentlemen, your money is no good here. If you get tired of Mr. Earp's good whiskey, the Cosmopolitan Hotel has an excellent restaurant. The rooms there are also comfortable and they are free of bedbugs and other night vermin."

Earp looked toward the open door, then back at Holliday. "I would appreciate it, Doc, if you would refrain from filling Pete Spence full of lead. We don't need problems with the Clantons right now."

Holliday smiled. "I only aim to relieve Mr. Spence of his money, not his life," he said, and left the table.

Watson stood up and pulled his hat low on his head. "I've had my share of milk curdle. Reckon I'll go along and get a room at the Cosmopolitan, since Mr. Holliday has recommended it so highly. You boys want me to register for you?"

Vent nodded. "We'll be along in a bit, Jim," and watched the Texan walk out the door.

"That feller own much of a spread?" Morgan asked.

"About half of Texas," the Preacher said, and stood up. "Mr. Morgan, if a man named Baldy Birch arrives in town, I'd appreciate your letting me know."

"A spot of trouble?" Morgan asked, watching the old gambler's face.

"A problem my nephew has. I and Vent are sorta tagging along."

"I've heard of Birch. Man's a cold-blooded murderer," Wyatt said.

"I've got a flyer over to the office on him," Morgan added. "A sheriff at Kelly, New Mexico's offering a thousand dollars for him, dead or alive."

"We're not after the reward," the Preacher said.

"I didn't think you were," Morgan countered, smiling faintly.

Rudy Timkins had been swaying with the buck and roll of the stagecoach for so long he began to wonder if he was at sea. Now, he stared morosely out the window at the barren landscape surrounding the cowtown of Benson and knew he was twenty-five miles from Tombstone.

As the coach rounded into the Butterfield stage station and the driver hauled the tired horses to a dust-stirring stop, several loungers strolled out to the edge of the sidewalk to see who was getting off today.

Timkins waited politely for the matronly wife of a Fort Hauchuca sergeant returning from visiting relatives in the north to alight, then brushed past a drummer who was struggling with three large display cases. Dropping into the hard-packed dust of the street, Timkins hitched his gunbelt into a more comfortable position and had his careful look at the loungers, decided they posed no threat to him and entered the cool confines of the station.

Walking to a counter presided over by a full-busted girl who Timkins guessed was probably half Indian, he bought two beef sandwiches and a large mug of coffee and sat at a table in the corner with his back to the wall. As he gulped down the food, a shadow fell across his table and he found himself staring into the sardonic eyes of Baldy Birch. Timkins stared back for a long moment, then returned to his sandwich, ignoring the former cavalry sergeant.

Birch grinned faintly, walked to the counter and said

something to the girl. Timkins saw her face redden, then she looked away and Baldy dug in his pocket and Timkins heard the soft jingle of coins as the big man placed a small stack of them in front of her. She slowly turned her head, glanced down, then reached a hand for the money, nodding toward the back of the building as Birch spoke softly to her.

Wheeling then, he passed out the door and Timkins saw him walk by a window toward the rear of the station. Looking back at the counter, he was in time to see the girl slip through a door. When Timkins turned his head and looked at the ticket agent, the man did not return his stare but instead gazed out a window as if the girl had never left.

The stage driver came in and said, "Five minutes, folks." Timkins finished his sandwich, entered a door marked "gents" and found the drummer struggling to get his pants fastened over a too-large stomach. When he came out, Timkins again looked for the girl, but she was still gone.

As the stage rolled away from the station, Timkins saw Birch come from behind the building and mount his horse, then fall in behind the coach, his lips pursed in a whistle.

The ticket agent glanced toward the lunch counter for the fifth time and then, irritated by the girl's continued absence, moved around his counter and through a door to the back of the building. He knew just where to look for her because she had pleasured him there more than once. Opening the door slowly, he stared in horror.

The girl was stark naked and covered with blood, her face a barely recognizable mask of cuts and bruises. Her breasts were marked by the slash of teeth and one nipple was missing. The insides of both her thighs were already turning purple as the clerk reeled away and vomited in a corner. Wiping his mouth with the back of his hand, he

ran from the room into the main station and shouted at a
startled man in a business suit, "For God sakes, go fetch
the marshal!"

Not waiting for an explanation, the man ran out and
returned in a few moments with a man wearing a star who
said, "What's all this about, Harold?"

Pointing a shaky finger, he said, "In there, marshal,"
and watched as the lawman unholstered his gun and walked
into the back room. By this time a crowd had gathered and
was trying to find out from the clerk what had happened.
Then they heard the marshal begin to curse in a low
monotone, and when he reappeared, he ordered someone
to go for the doctor and someone else to fetch a blanket
and a lady to assist.

"Somebody having a baby, Marshal?" one of the loungers asked, and snickered.

The marshal glared at him. "No, you damned fool.
Somebody almost killed Mary Running Doe; beat the poor
girl half to death," and he looked at the clerk and said,
"Harold, you didn't do that, did you?"

The clerk stared at the marshal in horror. "Oh my God,
no, sir. It was a big man . . . baldheaded . . . he gave
Mary some money and she went with him. . . ."

"Damned Injuns," the marshal said. "Ain't got no
morals nohow," and then a woman came in carrying a
blanket and asked, "Where's the lady having the baby?"

"Nobody's having a baby, dammit . . . begging your
pardon, Miz Brown," the marshal said. "Somebody done
beat the living hell outa Mary Running Doe. She's in the
back room."

Setting her mouth primly, the woman went through the
door, then a gurgling scream resounded, and all eyes
turned as the woman reappeared, holding on to the doorjamb.
"My Lord, Marshal May, who would do a thing like
that?" she choked out.

The doctor's appearance interrupted them, and the marshal and Mrs. Brown, her face white and her lips tight, followed him into the back room. Taking one look, the doctor said, "Marshal, best get a door in here so we can carry her down to my office. I can't work on her here."

May relayed the doctor's orders while Mrs. Brown carefully wrapped the blanket around the battered girl, who opened her eyes for a moment and said in a whimper, "Please . . . please . . . don't do that . . . don't . . ." then passed out again.

Looking at her, the doctor observed, "Now that was merciful."

When the door arrived, the doctor and the marshal carefully moved the injured girl onto its hard surface while Mrs. Brown tucked the blanket around her. Calling for two men, they carried her from the station. As she was moved along the street, a man and a young woman pulled in tired horses and sat watching the parade. After it passed the man leaned down and stopped a townsman wearing an apron and asked, "What's going on here, neighbor?"

"Some baldheaded gent raped and beat the hell outa Mary Running Doe down at the stage station," he said, and hurried off.

Looking at the green-eyed woman riding the blaze-faced sorrel, the man said, "That'll be Baldy Birch."

"Nice man," the woman said.

"One you don't ever want to be alone with," the man warned, and withdrew a sack of tobacco. The move revealed a deputy sheriff's star pinned on his left shirt pocket.

The marshal came back down the street from the doctor's office and, seeing the man and woman sitting their horses in the middle of the street, said, "I'm Marshal May; law around here."

The man nodded, said, "I'm Had Putnam, deputy sheriff up to Kelly, New Mexico. This here's Angel Brown. Her pappy owns the bank in Kelly.''

Looking at the ground, the marshal said, ''Long ways from home, ain't you?''

''Looking for a feller.'' Putnam watched the crown of the marshal's hat until the lawman looked up and asked, ''Anybody I can help with?''

'' 'Fraid not. Gent just visited you,'' Putnam said.

''Oh?''

''That was Baldy Birch who attacked the girl,'' the deputy said, and his mouth was a hard straight line.

''The hell you say? I've heard of him. Got a flyer on him at my office. Seems he's wanted for killing a lawman up to Hays, Kansas.''

Putnam nodded. ''He beat hell outa a saloon girl and the marshal rode after him. Shot the marshal dead.''

''You say you're looking for him?'' May asked.

''That's right . . .''

''What for?''

Putnam took a deep breath and said, ''He stuck up the stage on the Shakespeare run and lifted fifty thousand dollars. Got clean away after plugging the shotgun.''

''That's still outa your territory,'' May said, and waited.

''That money belonged to Miss Brown's father. It was bank loot recovered from three men who held up the Kelly bank and killed a couple of fellers. We caught them in Shakespeare.''

''I heard about that,'' May said.

''They's two things Birch enjoys. One's robbing folks and the other's beating hell outa women,'' Putnam told him.

Looking at Angel, who returned his stare with a pair of level green eyes, May observed, ''Funny thing for a woman to be doing—going along on a manhunt.''

''Her choice,'' Putnam said.

Shaking his head, May turned away, then stopped and said, "The gal Birch worked over was an Injun. Now usually folks around the San Pedro don't get too excited about Injuns, what with the 'Paches cutting up all the time, but Mary Running Doe was a sort of experiment. She went to school at the San Carlos Reservation and the folks at the Butterfield home office hired her to operate their grub counter. We sorta liked her around here. . . ."

"Reckon Birch must be heading for Tombstone," Putnam said.

"I reckon. The station clerk said he rode off after the stage."

"Probably rob the damn thing before it gets to Tombstone."

"If he does, he'll find Wyatt Earp and his brothers on his tail and they'll probably bring along Doc Holliday. He won't get far, and I'll promise you something else: he ain't getting away with what he did here neither, cause I'm gonna see if I can't take him. Feller like that deserves a necktie party."

"I'd be damn careful with Birch, I was you," Putnam counseled, and rode down street.

As Angel moved to follow, she smiled at May, and her face was suddenly transformed to one of striking beauty. The lawman gaped.

"Close your mouth, Marshal, you're attracting flies," Angel said, and rode away, her shoulders straight and her hips solid in the leather.

"Lord a'mighty," May said as he watched her ride off.

It was almost midnight and the shouts, gunshots and curses of brawlers still echoed down Allen Street. Vent lay on the unfamiliar bed and stared wide-eyed at the ceiling, cursing the idiots who had nothing better to do than run around wasting good ammunition and wearing out their lungs. He did not like to sleep under a roof. Somehow it always seemed to him as if he were in a jail cell. After spending most of his life sleeping under the stars, a hotel room was just too confining, particularly when the outside world sounded as if its britches had been burst in one long, thunderous rip.

"To hell with it," he said, and rolled free of the constraining blankets. Walking to the window, he looked down into Allen Street, marveling at the sea of miners, teamsters and cowboys who swaggered, staggered and lurched from saloon to saloon. A piano started up, then was suddenly silenced with a crash, followed by a wild shout and two gunshots. A man whirled through the door of the Crystal Palace Saloon clutching a gun in one hand and his stomach with the other. Reaching the middle of the wide thoroughfare, he turned, lifted the gun and fired five times through the swinging doors of the saloon. On the fifth shot, a shadow appeared in front of a barber shop and moved swiftly to where the gunman was reloading. Vent saw the flash of Wyatt Earp's long-barreled pistol rise and fall as he buffaloed the man. As the shooter hit the dirt facedown, a cowboy wearing chaps and a sombrero and holding a pistol burst through the door, only to find himself facing Earp's leveled gun.

The lawman's cold voice came clearly through Vent's open window. "Drop it or your next stop's hell!"

The man dropped the gun immediately and Earp said, "Back inside, and stay there."

The would-be gunman whirled and went back through the bullet-ripped door as Earp fastened a hand in the unconscious man's shirt collar and dragged him toward the sidewalk, where he stretched him out and examined his wound.

Virgil Earp stepped from Fifth Street, and, looking down

at the dark shadow lying at the edge of the walk, asked, "He dead?"

"Maybe. Caught one in the stomach, then I buffaloed him," Earp said. "Damn fool was throwing lead into the Crystal Palace."

A small crowd had gathered and Wyatt ordered them to carry the man to the doctor's office, then walked toward Fourth.

"Some job," Vent said as he strapped on his gun, buttoned his coat and let himself out in the hall just as the Preacher came from his room. Grinning at the old gambler, Vent said, "Hell of a place. Feller can't get sleep listening to that racket. Want a drink?"

Glancing over his shoulder toward Watson's room, the Preacher said, "Jim left about two hours ago. Followed him, figuring as hotheaded as he is he'd get himself in trouble."

"He back yet?"

"Nope."

"You know where he went?"

"Got his horse and rode north. Me, I followed him. He went up to the Diamond-D Silver and Cattle Company."

Vent stared at him. "The hell you say? Now why would he go and do that for?"

"Met a couple of fellers there," the Preacher said as they stepped out on the sidewalk.

"You recognize them?" Vent asked as a drunk staggered up and said gleefully, "Hell of place. You wanta fight?"

Before Vent could answer, the man's partner, considerably more sober than his pal, took him by the arm and said, "Come on, Al, let's find us some women," and led the belligerent one away.

"Feller sure's hell courtin' disaster," the Preacher said.

"You say you didn't know those gents that met with Jim?" Vent said.

"Didn't say that," the Preacher answered, pulling his hat low on his forehead and leading the way toward the Oriental, which was apparently still going wide open even though it was close to one o'clock. "Fact is, I think I know both of them. . . ."

Vent stopped and shook his head. "Sometimes, Preacher, you're as hard to get anything out of as a damned Papago Injun."

The Preacher smiled as he lit a cigar and blew smoke into the face of a passing drunk. "One of them fellers was Baldy Birch and the other fits the wanted dodgers on Rudy Timkins."

"Timkins? Hell, I thought they hanged him up at Prescott."

The Preacher shook his head. "If they did, his ghost's sure as hell healthy."

As they walked on, Vent thought about it for a long moment, then glanced at the Preacher and said softly, "Preacher, I'm sorry as hell about this."

"His paw wasn't no account and I reckon the boy took after him," the Preacher said, and led the way into the Oriental Saloon, where they found Doc Holliday sitting alone at a table near the back wall, a half-empty whiskey bottle in front of him. When he spotted them, he lifted his chin and Vent led the way to the gunfighter's table, nodded, said, "Long night, Doc."

"Sit down," Holliday invited, and Vent and the Preacher moved around to his side of the table and placed their backs to the wall.

The piano stool was empty, and on closer inspection Vent made out half a dozen bullet holes just above the keyboard. Looking at Holliday, he said, "Looks like the last of that piano."

"It's the last of the bastard who shot her up too," Holliday said morosely.

"Somebody plug him?" the Preacher asked as the bartender set two glasses in front of them.

Holliday poured for them, then shook his head. "No, as a matter of fact, nobody did; damned wonder though. The Irishman broke both his arms. Probably did him a favor. Anybody that dumb was bound to end up dead sooner or later if he kept packing a pistol."

"How'd the poker game go?" the Preacher asked.

"Broke about even," Holliday, who had won thousands of dollars during his gambling career, said.

"Some nights like that," the Preacher noted. "I was down to my spurs once. Had my horse, saddle, rifle and one forty-five in there, and then old Lady Luck, she done saw me sitting there about to go under and jumped on my back. I came away with my gear and more than twenty thousand dollars."

Vent smiled. "Up in Montana saw a feller gamble away a hundred-thousand-acre ranch and his wife one night and came back the next and win it all back. Funny thing though; when the other gent wanted to bet the wife again, the rancher refused to allow it."

Holliday grinned and the Preacher's eyes showed a faint twinkle as he watched the crowd. "How many men you reckon's in here?" he asked.

"About fifty or sixty," Holliday guessed.

"How much money will they drop in a night?"

Holliday looked at the Preacher, then said, "Oh, probably anywhere from five to ten thousand."

"We're in the wrong business, Preacher," Vent observed.

Holliday said suddenly, "Your nephew got a reason for talking to Baldy Birch?"

Vent and the Preacher stared at him. "Now how the hell did you catch on to that?" Vent asked softly.

Holliday shrugged. "I got a few people around. You fellers know Johnny Behan's got a man working for him named Anselamo Contreas?"

"We knew it," the Preacher said.

"Seems he was at the meeting between Watson, Birch and that mine owner, Colonel Alex," Holliday informed them.

"They was another man there too," the Preacher said. "Dirty-looking mutt named Rudy Timkins. I'd heard they stretched the little varmint's neck up at Prescott. Guess I heard wrong."

"Broke jail," Holliday told him laconically, tossing off his shot glass of whiskey and allowing Vent to refill it.

"The hell he did?" the Preacher grunted.

"Yep, broke out and left the jailer dead as a nit. Stole a horse and lit out for Kingman. Led old Del Bratton, sheriff from up to Prescott, one hell of a run, then shot his posse up and even managed to slip through a bunch of 'Pache headhunters."

Thinking about it, Vent realized they were now all together. He had no doubts as to who the colonel was. But what didn't jell was Jim Watson. Why was he meeting with the very men that hanged his friends and consigned him to Fredericksburg? If he ever went there . . .

Holliday had been watching him. Now he said, "Mr. Torrey, when you think it shows right through your head," and grinned as he lifted his glass and drained it off.

Turning to the Preacher, Vent asked, "Preacher, you got this figured yet?"

The Preacher shook his head. "Don't make sense."

Holliday looked toward the bar and said softly, "It does when you know the whole story."

Staring at him, Vent said quietly, "Doc, you got an ace in this thing?"

Holliday shook his head. "No, Mr. Torrey; no aces. I

do know who those fellers are though. That's the Bandera stranglers, or what's left of 'em.''

The Preacher lifted his drink and his hand was as steady as if he were thirty years younger. ''Here's to tricks and sneaks and their ultimate fate,'' he said, and they drank.

As they replaced the empty glasses on the bar, Sheriff Del Bratton, followed by a posse of eight men, pushed through the door and lined up along the wall.

''Hell among the yearlin's,'' the Preacher said softly.

Chapter 6

It was after midnight when Putnam and Angel pulled in their tired horses on a hill overlooking the cluster of buildings that was Tombstone. Allen Street, running east and west, was alive with lights, and lights showed as well from many of the buildings on side streets. As they sat and gazed down at the most infamous mining town in the West, the sound of music came faintly up the slope, then four slamming detonations echoed off the low hills surrounding the town as some roistering miner or cowboy cut loose with a forbidden gun.

"A damn rough town to take a lady to," Putnam said without looking at Angel, whose horse was getting restive.

"I understand the Cosmopolitan Hotel is a good, clean place to stop over," she countered. "I could use a bath and a night's rest on clean sheets."

The deputy led the way down the slope into Allen Street, then turned along a side street and onto Fremont, where Putnam asked a man on a bay horse directions to a livery stable.

"Down that-away," he said, pointing toward the OK

Corral, where a lantern over the entrance gate cast a dim glow into the street.

Putnam thanked him and, as he rode away, glanced back. The rider still sat his horse in the middle of the street staring after them, and Putnam was certain he was not the object of the cowboy's interest. Smiling faintly to himself, he led the way to the livery and went in search of the hostler, finding that worthy asleep in a chair. His snores literally rattled the windows of the small, one-room office.

Putnam woke him and made arrangements to stable their mounts, and as they started to leave the man said, "Friend, I don't know where you plan to stay, but I was you, I wouldn't escort the lady along Allen Street unless you're right sudden with that gun of yourn."

"We planned to put up at the Cosmopolitan," Putnam said.

"Why don't you try the San José House just down Fremont here? It's a clean place and a nice lady runs it," the liveryman counseled.

Putnam thanked him and started away in the direction he had indicated only to have the man call him back and warn him, "None of my business, mister, but they's a law agin totin' hoglegs in this here place. Marshal Earp has real strong feelings about that."

Putnam smiled and said, "It's all right, neighbor, I'm a lawman," and led Angel to the San José House, where she was immediately taken under the wing of a matronly lady who informed Putnam that unless Angel was his wife, she couldn't allow them to sleep beneath the same roof.

Bowing graciously, Putnam said, "I regret to say, ma'am, that Miss Brown is not my wife, but merely in my keeping. Her father is a friend of mine and we are in this fair city on business. I will make arrangements at some other establishment."

"Well, young man, you just be keerful down there on

Allen Street," she warned. "They's a whole passel of rascadallions hanging around them deadfalls who just love to rob strangers."

Putnam bowed again and said, "I thank you again, ma'am, but I reckon I'll be safe enough," and looking at Angel's wide-eyed innocent expression, thought: Damn, but she could fool a man out of his gold teeth.

After promising to return first thing in the morning and escort Angel to breakfast, Putnam left, walking carefully until he reached the Oriental, where he turned in with little more than whiskey on his mind.

The first thing he saw was a room full of men seemingly frozen to their chairs, their eyes on a big man standing just to the right of the door. Sensing a possible gunfight, Putnam immediately moved to his left only to find himself standing in front of four armed men whose hands were inches from their gunbutts.

When the fat man turned to look at him, Putnam grinned. "Long way from your feeding grounds, ain't you, Del?" he asked.

Bratton cocked his head to one side and observed, "Could say the same for you Had. Kelly, New Mexico, ain't just over the next hill."

A tall man sitting near the back of the room rose and Bratton turned sharply to look at him.

"Gentlemen, I'm Doc Holliday," he said. "This place belongs to United States Deputy Marshal Wyatt Earp. Now I'm sure if he were here, he'd invite you fellers for a drink. In his absence, I'll do it for him."

Bratton looked at Holliday for a long moment, then noticed the quiet man sitting near him, sided by a tall old man wearing black, whose cold distant eyes were watching Bratton and his men with what appeared to be mild interest.

Putnam moved up beside Bratton and said quietly, "Del,

the man you want ain't in this room, nor is the feller I'm hunting."

Holliday came down the room then and stopped in front of Bratton. "You'd be Sheriff Bratton from Prescott."

"I am." Bratton watched Holliday narrowly.

"I'm Had Putnam, deputy from Kelly, New Mexico," Putnam said.

Turning slightly, Holliday waved a hand at Vent. "The gentlemen at my table are Mr. Vent Torrey and the Preacher. You may have heard of them in your travels."

Bratton stared at Vent, seeing a quiet, brown-haired man dressed like any other range rider, his gray hat slanted slightly over his eyes and his only distinguishing feature an odd leather glove he wore on his right hand. The old man, Bratton knew, was a legend around the gold camps, but this was the first time they had crossed paths. Putnam walked past Bratton and went to Holliday's table, shook hands with Vent and the Preacher and turned to the sheriff. "I know these fellers, Del. Maybe you ought to come and join them and take advantage of Mr. Holliday's generosity."

Bratton looked over the crowd, then nodded once and moved to the table. His posse held their places, but accepted drinks when a waiter delivered them.

"Here's to hell and damnation," Holliday said, and tossed off his drink.

As he was refilling their glasses, the door opened once again and the tall, dignified form of Wyatt Earp entered, followed by a dandified-appearing man wearing a bowler hat and carrying a cane. He wore no coat and on his left hip a .45, its stag handle protruding at an odd angle toward his belt buckle, was snugged tight in a cutaway holster.

Holliday grinned as Earp and his companion moved down the room. Several men along the bar and at the card tables muttered a name at each other, then Earp stopped, and shaking hands with Bratton, said, "Welcome to

Tombstone, Sheriff Bratton.'' Nodding at his companion, he added, ''Gentlemen, meet Bat Masterson. An old friend of mine.''

Masterson looked at Holliday, then asked, ''Ain't they plugged you yet, Doc?''

Holliday looked off toward the bar, then back at Masterson and said mildly, ''No such luck, Mr. Masterson. Want you to meet some friends. Feller on your left is Had Putnam, deputy from New Mexico here on business. Big feller's Sheriff Del Bratton from Prescott. Also here on business.''

Pointing a thumb at Vent, Holliday said, ''This man is Vent Torrey,'' and Masterson, who had been nodding at each man as he was introduced, stopped and looked long at Vent, who returned his examination without expression. ''I've heard of you, Mr. Torrey,'' he finally said.

Holliday indicated the Preacher with a jerk of his blond head. ''If you don't know the Preacher, you ain't never turned a pasteboard.''

Masterson nodded gravely. ''Preacher, it's been awhile. We'll have to play a little poker while you're in town.''

''My pleasure, suh,'' the Preacher said.

The drinkers and gamblers had gone back to drinking and losing their money, but they were a great deal more quiet about it. Many of them would recall years later how five of the fastest gunmen in the West sat together in the Oriental Saloon and shared a bottle of whiskey.

''I suppose Mr. Torrey and the Preacher are here on business as well?'' Masterson asked innocently.

''As a matter of fact, they are,'' Holliday agreed.

As he lifted his glass, the door opened and a lanky boy wearing bib overalls came in, looked around, then went to Holliday's table and said, ''Excuse me, Mr. Holliday, sir, but can you tell me where I can find a man named Putnam?''

Putnam glanced at him and, noting his white face, felt a

cold hand reach inside of his stomach and begin to twist his insides as he said, "I'm Putnam."

The boy swallowed and stared around as if about to run, then said, "Mrs. Chance, over to the San José, said to run and fetch you, sir. She said to tell you to bring the marshal. She said somebody done ran off with that lady you left there tonight."

Putnam stood up and grabbed the boy by the arm. "Tell it, son. And calm down."

Almost stuttering now, the boy gulped out, "They come in and took her with guns, Mrs. Chance, she said."

"Damn," Putnam snarled, and wheeled toward the door.

Vent was on his feet too, as was the Preacher, and then Holliday spoke up. "Would you gentlemen mind explaining what's going on here? What lady are you referring to?"

Vent said, "Name's Angel Brown. Her daddy owns the bank in Kelly that got robbed." Looking at Putnam, he asked, "She come in with you, Had?"

"Yes, but it's a long story, Vent, and no time to tell it now," Putnam replied. "I'm going over to the San José House."

As one man, the group at the table rose and hurried from the saloon, followed by Bratton's posse. A lady had apparently been kidnapped, a hanging offense in Tombstone or any other town in the West.

Angel Brown was not afraid of the tall man with the military bearing. She was not afraid of the little gunman the others called Rudy. She was terribly afraid of the big man with the bald head and the strange eyes. They had blindfolded her shortly after leaving Tombstone, making her lie down in the back of the buggy. She had tried to estimate the distance they traveled by counting but halfway there lost track of her mental measurements when she felt the big man's hand caressing her thigh and snapped, "Stop that," and heard the tall man say mildly, "Baldy, you ain't changed a bit. Save that kinda stuff for the saloon gals. This is a lady we got here and I don't want her going back and telling folks we mistreated her."

The baldheaded man had merely laughed, but he took his hand away, and when they finally stopped and she was helped from the buggy, it was the one called Rudy who led her inside. Now she lay on a crude cot in a back room, and each time footsteps approached the door, she drew in her breath in fear it was the baldheaded one.

She did not know why they had taken her but assumed it was for ransom. She guessed someone had recognized her as a banker's daughter and tipped them and now they would hold her until her father paid for her release. As she thought of his reaction for just a moment, she regretted coming to Tombstone with Putnam. It just wasn't something a lone woman from a good family would normally do. She knew that. When they got home, and she refused to believe she wouldn't, tongues would wag. However, it was her father's money, and she had been entrusted with seeing that the funds were returned to the bank vault where they belonged.

Thinking of that now, she realized she was lying to herself, that she didn't give a hoot in hell about what people thought as long as she behaved like a lady and knew it. It was the pure excitement, more than anything else, that had brought her down the Tombstone trail after the stage was robbed. Putnam had said the holdup artist was a man called Baldy Birch and now he had her, and the money, and it was more excitement than she bargained for. She was not afraid of what her mother used to refer to as "a fate worse than death," but was in fact very curious about just what it was men and women did to cause all the snickering and rib punching that went on both in school

and among men she had watched hanging around the
mercantile in Kelly. She had spent enough time around
farm animals to know what the mechanics were but was
totally ignorant about the act as performed by humans.
Now, she thought, I may just find out in spite of myself,
and shuddered, abhorring the idea of intercourse with a
man like Baldy Birch. From him, her mind traveled to
thoughts of Vent Torrey, and thinking about him she could
easily conjure up his quiet face and probing brown eyes.
When he looked at her like that, she became all soft inside
and didn't know what to do with her hands or body. In
fact, she had the awful-wonderful feeling she was standing
before him stark naked, her body consumed with an inner
fire that threatened to ignite her. Rolling on her side
restlessly, she thought, what a simpleton you are. Here
you're being held prisoner, kidnapped by a bunch of
villains, and all you can think about is being naughty with
Vent Torrey.

Suddenly the door opened and the huge shape of Baldy
Birch blocked the light as he came into the room and softly
closed the door behind him.

"Hello, girlie," he said huskily.

"Go away," she snapped, staring at him as he came to
the side of the bed and gazed down at her. The moon was
slanting its rays through a barred window at the head of
the bed, sending a splash of pale light over her body and
reflecting from his bald pate.

"Me and you, honey, we're gonna have us a time,"
Birch said softly, and he sat down on the edge of the bed
and suddenly grasped her right breast in one huge paw.

"Don't, please don't do that," she cried as she tried to
move his hand. He was too powerful for her, and as he
pushed down on her breast, she could feel the swell of
muscle in his wrist.

Removing his hand suddenly, he stepped astraddle of

her, planted his knees solidly on each side of her body and ripped her blouse and her underclothing away in one tearing jerk, baring her full breasts to his hungry gaze.

"Damn you," she choked out, fighting him.

Then he came down on her full length and now his knee was forcing her thighs apart and she struggled with all her being but could not dislodge him. Slowly, inexorably, he forced her legs apart until she lay spraddled for his invasion. Reaching down below her waist, he grasped her underthings and ripped them away, leaving her lower body without even the protection of the flimsy garments she had worn.

"Oh, please God, help me," she cried out, trying to back toward the head of the bed in an effort to escape him. Then his belt buckle came loose with a clatter and struck her bare thigh, followed by his solid hips. As his naked flesh touched her, she shrieked and he laughed deep in his throat and said harshly, "Forget it, lady. The boys have gone. They ain't nobody here but me," and now he was trying to enter her body, and as the pain tore at her, she fainted for the first time in her life.

Vent led the small band of riders out of town, using the light of a pale moon to follow the buggy tracks freshly cut in the soft dirt of the road. Half a mile north of town, they turned off. He looked back at Holliday and Earp and asked, "What's west of here?"

"They's some mines. One of them, the biggest, belongs to Colonel Alex," Earp answered, staring off in the direction the buggy had taken.

"Alex, huh?" Vent mused, and then made a decision. "Maybe we should kinda split up just in case these fellers are smarter than we think and they try to double back on us. Mr. Holliday, could you and Mr. Earp swing on north a ways and then cut west toward this colonel's mine?"

"Little pincer movement, huh?" Earp mused.

"That's the idea," Vent agreed.

Bratton rode up beside Vent and said, "I'll take my boys and make a swing south and west," and glancing at Masterson, asked, "Mr. Masterson, do you know this country?"

"I've done some prospecting hereabouts," Masterson answered.

"Reckon you could go along with us and sorta make sure we don't get lost?" the sheriff asked.

Masterson smiled. "Be happy to, Sheriff," and he swung his horse in alongside Bratton's.

Vent glanced at the Preacher and then said, "I reckon me, the Preacher and Mr. Putnam can kinda drive straight on in to the mine, if that seems right to you fellers."

"Sounds good," Bratton said. "Let's get on with it, gents, we got a hanging to make arrangements for," and he followed Masterson into the darkness as Earp and Holliday drove north at a hard gallop.

Vent shook up the Appaloosa and led west along the wagon road, noting the deep cuts left by ore-wagon wheels and wondered why the former Major Alexander would be so foolish as to kidnap Angel Brown. Then Watson rode into the trail and Vent pulled up quickly and explained what had happened.

"You reckon these fellers stole the girl to use as bargaining goods?" the Preacher asked, speaking to Vent but watching his nephew.

"Don't know," Vent said, then looking at Watson, asked; "What you figure this is all about, Jim?"

Watson shook his head. "I ain't got the slightest idea. It's a tough nut to crack. Reckon we'll just have to play her by ear," and then they heard gunfire to the south.

"Sounds like Del ran into something," the Preacher said.

"Reckon we should maybe go check on him?" Putnam asked.

Vent thought it over then said, "No; he's a tough man and he's got him a tough posse. They should be able to handle just about anything that comes down the trail," and, lifting the Appaloosa into a trot, led the way on west.

Topping a low rise, Vent pulled in his horse and sat staring at the lights of a number of lanterns scattered among the dim shapes of buildings and mine head rigs in the distance.

"What you make that, Preacher, a mile?" he asked as the old gambler pulled his stud to a stop and had his look.

"More like three-quarters of a mile," he said.

Vent started to turn in the saddle to speak to Putnam when the shot tore the night asunder, its long lance of gun flame seemingly reaching out of nowhere to slam him from the saddle. Striking the ground on his back, he was amazed to discover that in spite of having been hard hit, he had drawn his gun somewhere between the saddle and the ground. Now he loosed four shots so fast they sounded like one and was rewarded when a high death shriek cut the blackness.

At the first shot the Preacher had wheeled his horse with a curse and, slamming the guthooks to it, leaped it clear of the top of the hill where they had been so obviously skylined. Vent heard him fire three shots from his .45s, then Putnam, who had dropped off his horse when Vent went down, cut loose, apparently fanning the gun hammer in one continuous roll, his bullets smacking into rocks and the ground and wailing away in a hideous death track across the night's darkness.

Half a dozen shots answered him and one of them put him afoot as it struck his horse somewhere in the body, driving a grunt from the animal. As Vent looked that way, he saw it slowly lean sideways, then fall heavily as Putnam dropped behind it and, reaching over its still-thrashing body, jerked his rifle free.

The Preacher disappeared into the darkness somewhere off to Vent's left, apparently attempting to whip-saw their unseen enemies in a crossfire. Reaching down to his side, he found a great splotch of blood and thought: Damn, I'm gut shot, and removed his hand, wondering how long he could remain conscious and still keep leaking blood and where the hell Watson had got to.

Then Putnam ran off to Vent's right and the Missourian heard him fire and someone scream and knew it was the last sound that bushwhacker would ever make. A shadow loomed up almost directly in front of him and he fired, heard the bullet tear through bone and flesh and saw the gunman reel away into the night, clutching his chest. Halfway down the slope the badly wounded man apparently lost his balance and fell the rest of the way, bringing a miniature rock slide down with him.

The Preacher's guns went off again and Vent moved south, taking advantage of the roar of the big .45s to hide his progress. As the old gambler laid down a sheet of lead, Putnam joined in with his rifle, and Vent thought, somebody is going to have to back off soon.

Putnam's rifle fell silent. Reloading, Vent thought. But then the deputy came walking toward him and Vent, not recognizing him at first, almost shot him. The moon's sudden appearance from behind a cloud was all that saved him.

"You all right?" Vent asked.

Putnam did not answer; instead he suddenly followed his buckling knees to the ground and rolled onto his back. Vent crawled quickly to his side and discovered he was staring into eyes that would never see again.

"He's up this way," a voice shouted, and Vent heard someone scrambling over the loose rock of the gentle slope and knew that he was in no shape to make a fight of it. Struggling to his feet, he leaned against the Appaloosa, got a firm grip on the saddle horn and somehow pulled himself into the leather just as the moon vanished behind its concealing cloud again.

Leaning far over the saddle, Vent walked the horse into the darkness, wondering how long it would be until they came after him.

"Vent?" the questing voice of the Preacher came from behind a large boulder.

"It's me," Vent said, and rode around to where the old gambler stood beside his horse. "I'm hit, Preacher . . . bad," Vent told him, and the Preacher came to him and checked his wound with probing fingers, then said quietly, "We better get the hell away from here. Where's Putnam?"

"Somebody else's riding his saddle tonight," Vent said grimly.

"Watson?"

"Don't know. He just sorta vanished when the shooting started," Vent said, knowing they were both thinking the same thing.

The Preacher mounted and asked, "Can you hang on?"

"I can make her," Vent vowed, but wondered how long it would be before he fell out of the saddle. "If I start to fall, Preacher, you rope me on. You hear?"

"All right," the Preacher promised, and took Vent's reins from his hand. "You just study on holding to that apple," and led the Appaloosa away into the night, angling southwest in hopes of crossing Bratton's trail.

Half an hour later, they rode into a narrow cut and Vent's horse almost stepped on a dead man's body. "Hold up, Preacher," he said softly, and when the gambler turned back he saw the body and dismounted. "It's one of Bratton's boys. Must have been ambushed here."

Far to the north the faint slam of guns firing rapidly

came to them and the Preacher looked that way, then said, "Reckon they've jumped Holliday and Earp. Now that was a mistake," and he mounted and led on through the cut, passing the sprawled shapes of five more dead men, whose faces gleamed still and cold in the moonlight. One of them was Del Bratton. When the Preacher spotted him, he pulled in and sat looking down and then said bitterly, "He was a damn good lawman. Somebody's gonna die for this," and moved on.

They had just cleared the pass when they heard the sound of hard-run horses coming from the north and Vent, feeling terribly weak now, said, "Better cut north and see if we can move behind them."

The Preacher dutifully swung off in a northeasterly direction as the rattle of hooves on hard ground passed to the west of them, then their riders pulled them to a dirt-scratching stop, and Vent and the Preacher could hear the sounds of voices but couldn't quite make them out.

They were some distance from Benson when another band of riders appeared suddenly on a hill to the west, their horses and riders standing stark and bold in the moonlight.

"Damn!" the Preacher exclaimed, and turned again, crossing the Benson-Tombstone road, then dropped down a steep bank and forded the shallow San Pedro River, moving east and north again.

Horses raced along the Tombstone road and Vent, who knew he must either tie himself to the saddle or fall off, wondered where the hell the colonel found all the men he apparently had.

"Preacher, you'd best tie me on this horse," Vent said, and the gambler stopped and got down. Coming back with a rope in his hands, he carefully strapped him to the saddle horn and the rear tiedown strings, then remounted wordlessly and moved on north.

They were following the general run of the river, but the Preacher knew that soon they would have to break away from it or get caught in a pincer move. Trying to think like their pursuers—and he knew they were being hunted—he figured they would cut his and Vent's tracks where they crossed the road and the river and be after them like hounds on a coon hunt. They'll give up some ghosts if they catch us, he promised himself, and kept going until a rider suddenly loomed before them and challenged, *"Quien es?"*

The Preacher drew swiftly but stopped midway between firing and holding the trigger at half pull and said softly, "Doc?"

"It's me," Holliday answered, and came alongside them as the Preacher holstered his .45. "Vent hit?" he asked, looking into the Missourian's face.

"I'm hit," Vent told him through gritted teeth. "Where's Earp?"

"He cut away from me when we ran into some riders. The bastards opened up on us, so we emptied a few saddles, then split up and made a run for it."

"We've got to get Vent to a doctor or he's gonna bleed to death on us," the Preacher said.

"Nearest town's Dragoon," Holliday said, and added, "Old man Keppler's a doc and pretty good if you can catch him sober. Works on gunshot wounds real handy."

"How far's Dragoon?" the Preacher asked.

"About five miles from us now," and Vent marveled at how far they had come. He knew they would soon be riding in morning's light and told Holliday, "If we get caught in daylight, we're dead."

"He's right," Holliday agreed, looking at the Preacher.

"Then let's head for Dragoon," the gambler growled, and led Vent's horse north, following closely behind the dentist.

False dawn was upon them when their luck ran out. As they forded a narrow tributary of the San Pedro, half a dozen riders burst from a tangle of brush and opened fire.

The Preacher and Holliday drew like twin demons and shot three men loose from their saddles in less than four seconds, then the gambler dropped the Appaloosa's reins and drew his second gun, firing first one and then the other as the riders broke for cover. One man's horse bolted wildly, and as he passed Holliday, the deadly dentist snaked a knife from his breast pocket and slashed the gunman's throat from ear to ear, pitching him from his mount as a great gout of blood poured down his horse's shoulder.

Vent had drawn his gun at the first enemy shot and now he got off two rounds and cursed when they missed a fleeing rider. The Appaloosa, spooking at the lack of control, suddenly ran northeast, reins trailing on the ground.

Vent saw Holliday race his horse into a pile of rocks, pursued by two men, who within seconds lay dead on the ground, shot through the head and the body. The Preacher was riding in a southerly direction, firing over his shoulder at five men who leaned far over their horses' necks and laid down a murderous sheet of lead, only to miss the Preacher cleanly when he suddenly swerved his horse and leaped the big stud over a tangle of thorn brush to vanish from view. Then Vent's horse carried him beyond the fight and he lost consciousness for several minutes, swaying wildly in the saddle.

When he regained consciousness, he was far to the north and the Appaloosa was still running. Noting the tangled rocks and brush they were dodging through, Vent, fearing the big horse would go down, managed to bark out an order and was gratified when the Appy slid to a sudden stop, almost tearing Vent loose from his bindings. Leaning forward, he tried to reach the reins, then realized the horse had apparently stepped on them and torn them from the bridle. Kneeing him, Vent clucked and the Appy stepped out lightly as full daylight came to the desert, the sun's rays lancing onto the sand from its perch on a hilltop to the east.

Later, Vent could not remember how long he was on the horse, but when the animal finally stopped and Vent looked up from pain-filled eyes, he was in front of a battered shack with smoke drifting lazily from a rusty stovepipe to disperse in the early morning air. A horse nickered from a corral to the east of the shack and the Appy answered with a soft gurgling sound, then the door of the house opened and Vent was gazing into the bores of a double-barrel shotgun in the hands of an Indian woman.

He stared at her for a long moment, then finally croaked out, "Waste of time, lady. I'm already shot all to hell."

She came to him and lifted a hand to touch the great splotch of blood on his shirtfront, then untied the ropes and, as Vent slid off the Appy, caught him and helped him into the cabin. It was as mean looking inside as outside, but there was a bed and she helped Vent to it, lowering him carefully so as not to bump his wound. Touching him lightly on the shoulder, she said in excellent English, "I'll find a place to hide that horse of yours, cowboy," and went away.

Vent awoke to a feeling of coolness against his side and, looking down, saw the woman had removed his shirt, pants and boots and was washing away the blood from his wound.

"How bad?" he asked.

"Bad enough," she said, her brow furrowed in concentration. Vent looking at her closely, saw she was a handsome woman with a narrow face and large eyes. Her lips were full and mobile and her hair, unlike most Indian women, had been carefully combed and fastened back with a metal brooch. She caught him staring at her and smiled.

"You like how I look?" she asked, and Vent tried to smile back but found it hurt. "I like how you look," he said, then asked: "You got water?"

Nodding, she rose and brought him a tin cupful and he drank it down, then wondered if he was gut shot.

"If I'm shot through the guts, that ain't gonna help," he said.

"An old wive's tale." She shrugged, then added, "The bullet went through your side and out the back. It missed the bones, but you got a hell of a big hole there, cowboy. You ain't gonna be riding for a while."

"What's your name?" he asked.

"Noona," she said, then looking at him, added: ":I am Apache."

Amazed that she would help him, he asked curiously, "Why help a white eyes?"

"I sell my body to white eyes so why shouldn't I help one," she answered simply, and then grinned. "I am a whore. Does that bother you?"

"No, ma'am," Vent said. "Don't make me no mind what a human does for a living as long as they do their best," and then realized what he had said and looked into her eyes as she grinned impudently at him and declared, "Don't worry cowboy, I do my best," and rose and went outside, carrying the bloody water. He heard her dump it in back of the shack and realized she was smart enough to know that if he was shot someone must be looking for him so don't leave any evidence around. He wondered what she would do if they came to the cabin.

When she came back in he asked, "What will you do if someone comes here looking for me?"

"Will they?" she asked, arching her eyebrows and pursing her lips.

"They may. It's according to where I'm at . . . ."

"Just to the east of Dragoon. The law looking for you?"

"No lady, it ain't the law. I made me some enemies and they'll be ahunting."

"If they come, what will you do?" she asked, staring at him.

It was then he remembered his gun. "My gun. What happened to it."

She smiled. "There." She pointed to the head of the bed. He saw it hanging in its holster from a bedpost and was relieved. "I reloaded it," she said simply, letting him know she was aware he had shot at someone.

It hurt when she carefully raised his waist to pass the bandage beneath him, and when she tied it he almost passed out. Now he lay quietly staring at the ceiling as she bustled about the cabin. "My horse? He all right?"

"Up in the rocks. I hid him. No one will find him."

"They'll find me and they may kill you for hiding me," he told her, and waited.

Returning to the bed, she looked long at him, then asked, "Can you walk if I help you?"

"I can walk," he said, but wouldn't have bet a plugged Mexican peso whether he could actually stand up, let alone walk.

Helping him off the bed, she slung his gunbelt over her shoulder, then retrieved his shirt, pants and boots and said, "Put your weight on me, cowboy. We're going for a little walk. It isn't far, but it's uphill," and she helped him from the cabin. Outside he was suddenly attacked by a sharp spell of dizziness, then it went away and he gritted his teeth and, taking one step after the other, allowed her to guide him up a narrow path and around a bend in the rocks where a cave suddenly appeared, its black maw cool and inviting. Inside she lowered him on a mattress and lifted a blanket over him and said, "I'll bring some water and food, then you must sleep."

After she left, he looked around in the dim light and saw she had brought his saddle and gear into the cave and guessed the Appy must be close by.

He was asleep before she returned.

Angel awoke to the sound of a loud argument and for a long moment had trouble orienting herself, then it all came back to her with a rush. Looking down, she saw someone had thrown a blanket over her. The door to her prison was partially open and through it she could see the hulking shape of Baldy Birch staring belligerently at someone across the room.

Whoever it was spoke: "Damn you to the darkest depths of perdition, Baldy. You're insane, you know that? Here we got this thing all tied up and Watson's friends practically nailed down in a pine box and you try to rape a banker's daughter. . . ."

"My business," Birch snarled.

"Your business, hell," the other man in the room snapped. "You're fixing to get all our necks stretched. Dammit man, you know where that sorta thing ends."

"Hell, just kill the girl and her mouth's shut forever," Birch said carelessly.

There was a long silence, then the other man asked softly, "What monstrous thing did a woman do to you to get you to hate them all so much?"

Birch whipped around and said viciously, "None of your damn business, Colonel. You keep pushing at this and you'll end up pushing something else, only it'll be daisies on your grave."

"Why you idiot! You'd kill me over a girl? My God, I always knew you were completely insane, but I didn't realize until now how damn stupid you were."

Birch cursed, then turned and walked from Angel's view, apparently opening a door somewhere as he said, "I'm gonna take me a little ride and see what them so-called hardcases of yours has got done. By now that gunfighter, Leatherhand, and his rusty old gambler friend should be good and dead."

Before the second man could answer, the door closed, then a shadow blocked the light and someone came to her bedside and a voice asked, "You awake, miss?"

"Why are you holding me?" she asked.

"I'm sorry about Birch. I . . . I stopped him before he could hurt you," the man said, and Angel, looking up at him, noticed how tall he was.

"I don't know. I fainted," she said.

"He won't bother you again," the man promised. "If he does, I'll kill him and he knows it."

"He said he wanted to kill me," she told him.

"Talk. Ain't nobody going to harm you. When this is all over, you'll be released. Meanwhile, you just stay in here and don't get nosy. Some of us can't afford to be seen by you. You understand?"

Angel knew what he meant. See his face; be able to identify him, he'd have to kill her. "I understand," she said.

"Good girl. Now, you, you're just bait on a trap. The trap's been sprung. You'll be released soon," and he turned and left.

For a long time she lay listening to the sounds from outside. Several riders rode in and left again, their horses' hooves pounding off in the night as men called to each other. Once she heard a man groaning, apparently badly wounded, then silence. She thought he must have passed out or died. Men came and went in the other room, but she did not recognize their voices.

Then the door opened and a woman came in carrying a

tray. Walking to her bedside, she sat it on the nightstand and said, "I hope you can eat in the dark, honey, 'cause the boss says no lights."

"What is it?" she asked huskily, then realized she was not only ravenously hungry but badly in need of a drink of water. "Do you have some water?"

"There's a full pitcher here," the woman said, and Angel heard her pour a glassful. A hand extended in the pale light and she took the glass and drained it and asked for more. The meal was beef, eggs and biscuits, drenched in heavy gravy . . . and delicious. Within five minutes her plate was clean and the second glass of water gone. "Can I have some more?" she asked.

The woman chuckled and, picking up her plate, left the room, returning a few moments later with a second helping. "If you need the bathroom, it's through that door." The woman pointed to a closed door in the far wall.

Thanking her, Angel attacked the food as the woman lingered, then asked, "Did . . . did Baldy . . . uhhh . . ."

"No, he didn't. But it wasn't from not trying. That man in the other room, the one Birch called colonel, I guess he arrived in time to save my virtue."

"Did it need saving?" the woman asked, and Angel detected bite in the question.

"If you mean, am I chaste, the answer is yes, why I don't know. I've spent my life around men and that's all they seem interested in."

Now the woman laughed and, still chuckling, went away. Angel wondered who she was, but decided she was probably some kind of camp follower to these outlaws and rose and sought the bathroom. When she finished and started to leave the room, she noticed a faint light coming through a crack and, looking closer, decided it must be the moon. Pushing against the boards, she was startled to discover there was give to them. Returning to the small bedroom, she searched until she found a broom in a corner. Carrying it, she returned to the bathroom and, moving very cautiously, inserted the end between the boards and began to pry. Suddenly the board popped and fell away from the building, hitting the ground below where she stood and sliding down an incline. Holding her breath, she waited for someone to burst into the room, but apparently no one heard the sound of the falling board so she went to work on the second one. When it came away, she was ready and grabbed it before it could fall, carefully leaning it against the outside of the building. Checking the size of the aperture she had made, Angel decided it was large enough to allow her passage. Quietly returning to the other room, she carefully arranged the blanket so that it appeared as if a human shape lay there, thinking the lack of light in the room was in her favor, and within moments was outside and creeping away from the shack.

She walked for about two hundred feet, then circled the scattered outbuildings searching for a corral and a horse. She was just passing a tall, odd-shaped structure when a powerful arm snaked from its doorway and, muffling her outcries, jerked her inside.

"Going somewhere, baby?" Baldy Birch chuckled as his hands began roving over her body.

She sagged in his arms, and thinking she had passed out again, he laughed deep in his throat. "That's all right with me, little lady. At least, the colonel won't bother us here," and he started to lower her to the floor when she jerked away and grabbed for the door as he lunged after her, cursing wildly.

Instead of the doorknob, her hand fell on a cross-member along the wall and suddenly she had a hammer in her hand and was whirling toward him. Unable to stop his charge, he ran full into her savage down-swinging blow. It struck him squarely in the forehead, and grunting, he reeled backward and suddenly dropped from view, his voice ripping loose in an awful scream that was confined to the narrow mine shaft he had toppled into. She heard his body slamming into cross-beams and the sides of the shaft seemingly forever, then he struck the bottom with a loud thud and Angel guessed he had probably landed on top of an iron ore car. Leaning against the wall, hammer still clutched in her hand, she took great gulps of air and waited for someone to open the door, but apparently the shaft had muffled Birch's dying screams for no running footsteps and no cries from the house cut the darkness.

It required a good twenty minutes for her to find the corral and saddle a horse, and then she was riding south at a slow walk, the lights of the mine growing dimmer with distance. When she felt it was safe, she lifted the animal to a fast trot and rode toward the dim lights of Tombstone, just showing along the distant horizon.

Johnny Behan sat in his office and brooded. He had long ago accepted the fact he must do something about the Earps. Before they arrived in Tombstone, things were coming together and the name of the game was money and lots of it. Now, with Wyatt Earp and that crazy dentist gunfighter Doc Holliday hanging around wearing badges and acting like lawmen, he couldn't even attempt to carry out the task he had been assigned.

In Tucson, they were getting nervous.

He looked up as the door swung open and Ike Clanton swaggered in, sprawled out in a chair and rolled and lit a cigarette, blowing smoke in Behan's face.

Staring at him distastefully, Behan observed, "Some day, Ike, somebody's gonna fill you plumb fulla lead."

"I reckon, but they ain't did her yet," the rancher countered.

The two men were old acquaintances, although nobody

who knew them would go so far as to say they were friends. They needed each other. That was all.

Behan was sheriff of Cochise County. Ike Clanton and his family ran a ranch east of Charleston they used as a cover for running stolen beef up from Mexico and peddling it to the army to feed the penned-up Apaches on the San Carlos Reservation. Ike and his brothers were also stage robbers, taking a continuous cut from the bullion shipped out of the area by the miners.

Ever since the Butterfield stage line had hired that hothead Morgan Earp to ride shotgun on the Tombstone-to-Tucson run, it had been worth a man's life to try and stand it up. Some had tried, only to wind up blown all over the landscape by Morgan's deadly shotgun.

Looking at Ike, Behan said, "You know, Clanton, we've let those damn Earps take over Cochise County. Hell, look at them. Wyatt's a U.S. marshal, Virgil's city marshal and Wyatt's his assistant; James runs that damn saloon of theirs and backs them on every play they make and even James, as easygoing as he is, is nobody to trifle with."

"Ah hell, James ain't no problem," Clanton said. "Him with that lame arm. Can't do much."

"Then there's Doc Holliday," Behan said softly.

"Me, I'm gonna fill that damn dude so fulla holes, he'll sound like a church organ every time the wind blows," Clanton vowed.

"More like he'll put a bullet in you or slit your throat and that'll be the end of Ike Clanton," Behan said dryly.

"He's overrated. Just because he bumped over a few drunks and saloon swampers don't make him the big shuckins around here."

"Sure," Behan said sarcastically. "Holliday's put twenty five drunks and swampers in the ground. Like hell he has and you know it, Ike. Don't dally with that man. He'll kill you for sure."

"If I can't do it alone, I'll get Billy and Phin and the McLaurys to help me," Clanton said.

"Sure you will, Ike, and you'll all be dead. You start up with Doc and you'll have the Earps to handle."

Ignoring him, Clanton asked, "You know this feller, Leatherhand?"

"I know him," Behan said grimly. "He's the one gent who could take Doc and probably the Earps to boot."

"I've heard of the Preacher," Clanton mused. "He's gettin' a little long in the tooth for pistol fighting."

"Don't bet your life on it," Behan cautioned. "That old man's as dangerous as a rattler when you poke him up. Remember, it was him and Owney Sharp and Cam Spencer who helped Leatherhand in that fight with the Denver big-money boys."

Both men turned to stare out the window as a rider on a lathered horse spun onto Tough-Nut Street and turned in sharply in front of the courthouse.

As the rider leaped down, Behan said, "Now what the hell?"

Pushing through the door, the man said, "Hell's to pay up north, Johnny. Been a big gunfight. Looks like Del Bratton and his whole posse's dead, drygulched in a canyon west of the Greenhorn Mine. . . . That ain't all," the rider continued. "Somebody found that New Mexico deputy over near the colonel's mine. He was dead as hell. They hauled the body into Dragoon."

Behan, never one to pass up an opportunity, rose and said, "Them damned Earps and Holliday have gone crazy. Looks like they've killed these lawmen in order to escape punishment."

"What punishment?" the rider asked, staring at the sheriff.

"Why hell, them law officers had warrants for all three Earps and Holliday," and turning to Clanton, he ordered,

"Ike, go find Pete Spence and Frank Stilwell. We're gonna form a posse and run down the Earps and Holliday. They'll swing for this."

As Behan led the way into the street, they met Billy Claibourne, and Ike said, "Come along, Billy, we're going after the Earps."

Looking at Behan, Claibourne asked, "What the hell's going on here? Earp's a U.S. marshal. Johnny, you want the whole damn army down here from Fort Hauchuca?"

"Won't happen," Behan snapped, legging it for the OK Corral and his horse. "Them Earps done went crazy and killed the sheriff from Prescott and another lawman from New Mexico," and he repeated his story of the warrants as Claibourne listened in amazement.

"Can we prove it?" he asked.

"Hell, who needs to? Those boys, they'll be riding a cloud by sundown and our problems with the Earps will be over."

As the posse mounted up in the street in front of the OK Corral, Camillus Fly came from his photography studio and approached Behan. "Sheriff, all right if I tag along?"

Not wanting a record of what he planned for the Earps, Behan said, "Not this time, Cam. We're dealing with some damned dangerous men and they've recruited that feller Leatherhand and the Preacher. It could get pretty bad."

Fly stared at him. "Wait a minute, Behan. Everybody knows Vent Torrey is square. Hell, he wouldn't be involved in this."

"Not my information," Behan said, and wheeled his horse away, shouting: "Let's ride, boys. We got us some outlaws to catch," and raced north along Fremont Street.

Watching them disappear, Fly shook his head, then looked up when Clum came across the street and asked,

''Where's our brave and glorious crime fighter off to this morning?''

''Says he's gonna go round up the Earps and Doc Holliday,'' Fly said. ''Claims they killed Del Bratton and that feller Putnam from up New Mexico way.''

Clum laughed. ''As usual old Behan's gone off half cocked again. Hell, Doc and Wyatt been over to the Oriental in an all-night poker game. They couldn't have shot anybody.''

''Well, I'll be damned.'' Fly chuckled gleefully. ''Old Behan's face's gonna be red on this one. . . . That calls for a good breakfast. How about joining me over to the French Restaurant. I feel like celebrating.''

''My pleasure.'' Clum laughed and the two men walked away.

Chapter 7

Anselamo Contreas returned to Tombstone early on a Sunday morning, finding the town unusually quiet even for that time of day. A vain man, the slim, delicate-featured Mexican from Texas wore a black suit with silver trimming, a wide, black sombrero and a vest to match. His pistol hung in a flower-stamped holster trimmed in silver and semiprecious stones. Even the shells filling the loops on his gunbelt had been polished to a high gleam. The silver-mounted spurs adorning the heels of the fancy butterfly boots he had had shipped up from Mexico City where the greatest bootmakers in the world plied their trade were worth six months of any cowboy's pay.

Between his knees, a powerful white horse walked with high delicate steps along the length of Allen Street and, when a lop-eared dog came sniffing at its heels, let drive one steel-shod hoof into its ribs, tossing it effortlessly along the street and against a water trough where it lay kicking feebly.

Contreas turned in his black silver-trimmed saddle, looked once at the dying dog and rode on with a shrug.

On his left breast he wore the badge of a deputy sheriff, its glitter almost lost amid all the other silver the Mexican wore.

As he passed the Oriental Saloon, he turned his head and laid a cold, unblinking black-eyed stare at Doc Holliday, who leaned against a porch support chewing on a porcupine-quill toothpick.

"Doc." The Mexican deputy nodded gravely.

"Señor Contreas," Holliday answered just as gravely.

Pulling the beautiful white horse to a stop, Contreas rounded on Holliday and spoke softly to the animal and was rewarded when it remained almost motionless. "How have things been in Tombstone?" he asked.

"Fine as frog's hair, el Jefe," Holliday replied.

Contreas grinned. "Then I am happy I stayed away two weeks instead of one," he said.

"Get your prisoner delivered all right?" Holliday, not really caring one way or the other, asked.

"That was very sad, Señor Doc," Contreas, who spoke perfect English, said mournfully.

Holding up his hand, Holliday said, "No, let me guess . . . The feller tried to pull a sandy on you and you just naturally had to plug him. Right?"

"I'm afraid so." Contreas grinned, then, looking past Holliday, said, "Ah, good morning, Marshal Earp. I trust you had a good night's sleep?"

Earp smiled slightly and observed, "As a matter of fact, I stayed up all night playing poker, but now that you're back in Tombstone, we'll all sleep sounder in our beds."

"So be it." The Mexican nodded and, clucking at the big white horse, barely touched the reins and was gone along the street, his back ramrod straight.

"Feisty little banty, ain't he?" Earp observed.

"Someday, Wyatt, I'm gonna slit that greaser's guzzle just to watch him bleed," Holliday promised.

"Ummm . . . The Preacher rode in half an hour ago. Said he looked all over hell for Vent, but lost his trail over east of Dragoon somewhere."

"Well, that tells us Vent got away or they took him," Holliday said slowly. "If he'd piled off his horse out there, the Preacher sure as hell would have found him or that Appaloosa."

Glancing along the street, Earp said, "Heads up. Looks like our sheriff has returned to the fold and he's brought Bratton and Putnam along with him."

Earp stepped back inside the saloon, then reappeared, leaning against the wall near the door as Behan pulled his tired horse to a stop and sat glaring at Holliday.

"Holliday, you and Earp have gone too far this time," he said loudly, glaring around as several businessmen came from just-opened stores to stand and watch a possible confrontation.

"Mind telling us what we're supposed to have done?" Earp asked.

Pointing at the dead men slung over saddles, Behan shouted, "Why you murdered these poor lawmen, and them out to do their duty and serve murder warrants on you men. Now me and this here posse's gonna have to arrest you two, Earp, and by God, you'll hang for it."

Ike Clanton rode forward and, staring belligerently at Holliday, snarled, "To hell with all this palaver. Let's haul these boys in and take 'em on down to the OK and string 'em up to the gatepost."

"My, ain't he bloodthirsty," Holliday observed without taking his eyes off the posse.

Then Earp stepped to the edge of the sidewalk and looked at Behan for a long moment. "Either you're a complete idiot, and I suspect you are, or you're a bold-faced liar, Behan. We have a dozen witnesses, including

Mr. Clum and the judge, who saw us sitting in the saloon all night playing poker.''

''Besides,'' Holliday observed mildly, ''if you fellers start the ball bouncing here, I'm gonna drop you, Behan, then that loudmouthed cowboy son of a bitch, Ike Clanton, then the rest of you can have at her.''

''I'll put Pete Spence and Billy down, and Virgil, he's hunkered behind the door there, he'll just naturally blow old Phin right into hell with that Greener he's aiming at him,'' Earp said, and, hands close to his gunbutts, waited.

Behan knew when the deck was stacked against him. Glaring at Earp, he said, ''Someday, Mr. Earp, you are going to get your comeuppance, by damn, you are.''

''If I do, it'll be by a better man than you are, Johnny Behan,'' Earp vowed.

''Gents, I'm getting thirsty,'' Holliday said suddenly, and now his voice was no longer bantering. It had taken on an unmistakable cold, deadly quality.

''Come on boys,'' Behan said, ''They'll be another time,'' and he led his men down the street and around the corner of Fourth and off toward Fremont.

Vent awoke to darkness and lay still for a long moment as he tried to remember where he was and what had happened to him. His side ached atrociously. He knew he must be running a very high fever for his body was drenched with sweat. When he raised his hand to wipe it from his face, he discovered he had barely enough strength to get it halfway up his body.

''You are awake,'' a soft voice said, and Vent strained into the darkness, trying to find the person behind the voice.

''You've been very sick for several days,'' the voice said again, and then it all came back with a rush. The Indian woman called Noona, the chase, being ambushed and shot, the cave and the days of falling in and out of the black maw of the fever as it raged through his body, slowly sapping his strength and his will to live. Now it had broken, the woman said, but he wondered about the wound. Had it become infected? He had known men to die of an infected wound after the fever seemed to leave them.

"How is the wound?" he asked.

"It is getting better, but I cannot stop the pain of healing, only the pain of dying," she said.

"You used Indian potions?" He was no stranger to the ways of Indian medicine. He had watched his Ute friend, Swift Wind, greatest shaman of all the Ute tribes, work miracles with roots and herbs.

"Yes, I used the Apache medicine," she said.

"My horse? He is cared for?"

"Ah, just like a great warrior. He thinks of his horse first," and she laughed softly and said teasingly, "I will feed you some broth soon. I hope you like it. I call it Appaloosa soup."

Vent was amazed. Very seldom had he ever met an Indian—particularly an Apache—with a sense of humor, leastways one a white man could fathom. "He was very fat," he countered. "He should have made excellent soup."

He heard her laugh softly again as she walked to the cave entrance and pulled back a blanket, sending a shaft of sunlight into the rocky cubicle and forcing Vent to close his eyes for a moment. When he opened them, he was staring up at a tall Apache brave. The Indian looked down on him for a moment, then squatted and, picking up Vent's tobacco from a nearby rock outcropping, calmly rolled a cigarette and lit it with a large kitchen match he dug from somewhere beneath the ragged red shirt he wore. Taking a deep pull, he handed it to Vent and said, "It's no peace pipe, but it'll do until one shows up."

Noona gestured toward the handsome brave and said proudly, "This is my brother. He speaks the white man's language as if born to it, does he not?"

"He does," Vent said. "The San Carlos?"

The Indian nodded. "Mr. Clum, he was the agent then. A good man. Now he gives the people of Tombstone sheets of the written white man's language each week and many of them hate him for it. He should have stayed at San Carlos. He was loved there."

"You became renegade when he left?" Vent asked, knowing no Apache who walked away from the agency did so unless he had run away or could prove he was an Indian policeman.

"I became free again," the Indian said, then tapping his chest lightly, declared, "I am Deerslayer, second cousin to Vitorio, leader of the Chircahua Apaches."

"I am Vent Torrey."

"I know you." The Indian nodded his head. "You are the one called Leatherhand. Even the Chircahuas know of you, for you have killed their brothers in the northern country. They say you are a great warrior."

"I am a badly wounded warrior now."

Noona came and laid a hand on her brother's powerful shoulder. "He must sleep, brother. He needs rest. Such a great warrior should not die in a cave with the bats. He is one who must go to the Star Maker from the back of his war horse in combat with other brave men."

Deerslayer rose and walked to the cave entrance, then stopped. "They seek your life all through these hills, but if they travel into the Dragoons, they forfeit their own for Vitorio awaits them," and he laughed deep in his throat and was gone. The girl followed and Vent was alone once more.

He closed his eyes and was immediately asleep.

Vent slept for two days, coming back to the reality of

the cave and his wound only momentarily while his body caught up on sleep. Each time he opened his eyes the Indian girl was sitting at the foot of his bed. She would walk to a water container and bring him a dipper of icy spring water, hold it while he gulped it down his parched throat, then watch as he dropped off again.

Just before dark on the second day he awoke to the sounds of horses' hooves down by the cabin and sat up, reaching for his holstered pistol. While buckling it around his naked waist, he discovered he had regained considerable strength, but when he tried to stand, he had to move carefully to the cave wall and cling to the rock as he worked his way to the entrance. Pausing there, he took several deep breaths, then slipped out past the hanging blanket and, still bracing himself on boulders, worked his way along the trail until he had a clear view of the cabin.

Four men sat horses down there. Noona, her head on one shoulder, eyes wide and inquiring, gazed up at them. One of the men said harshly, "You see a big man on a Appaloosa horse come this way, whore?"

Noona shrugged. "No speak white man's tongue. No speak."

Vent looked the riders over but did not recognize them, although a lean auburn-haired man with a saturnine expression on his face and two guns at his hips looked vaguely familiar.

One of the men tipped a thumb at the lean one and asked, "You know who this man is?"

Again Noona shrugged.

"He's Johnny Ringo and he doesn't like being lied to."

Ringo glanced around uneasily and Vent, having lived by the gun long enough to know the feeling of being watched, guessed the Ringo Kid, as he was called, was feeling it now. Carefully, Vent lowered his head beneath the top of the rock and waited.

"You try hiding this here feller and we'll come back and scalp ya," the man who had introduced Ringo said.

"Ah hell, Rudy, she don't know nothing," someone else put in, and Vent carefully looked over the rock again, but this time he had the big .44 in his fist just in case Ringo's intuition caused him to look up the trail.

"I don't give a damn about this here Injun whore," Timkins said. "I just figure we should take a look at every side of this damn coin. We've run out trails all over hell and still no Leatherhand."

A short, squat man nudged his horse forward and snarled, "Dammit, Ringo, Rudy's right. This here jigger just couldn't up and disappear. He has to be somewhere."

Nodding his head toward the distant Dragoons, Ringo said, "He's probably up there, and if he is, he won't last long. Hell, he's got lead in him. He left a passel of blood at the ambush. He won't be in any shape to take care of himself. By now he's Apache bait."

"Apache? I Apache," Noona said.

Timkins looked down at her for a moment, then asked without turning, "Any of you boys want some of this?"

"Not me," the squat man said. "Danged Injuns smell."

Ringo laughed and, turning his horse, led the way down the canyon. As they passed through the narrow rock cut leading to the cabin, Vent saw Deerslayer rise up above them and level a Winchester and held his breath, but the Indian did not shoot and the men rode around a bend and were gone. Glancing toward Vent's hiding place, Deerslayer held the rifle above his head and grinned hugely. Vent waved back, then suddenly sat down . . . hard.

He heard the Indian say something in a sharp, carrying voice, then the girl was helping him back to the cave on wobbly legs and Vent managed to hold onto his consciousness until he reached the bed. Darkness seized him just as the sun dropped beyond the horizon and plunged the hidden cabin, rock canyon and cave into near night.

For two weeks Vent convalesced and fretted, then he looked up from a game of solitaire he was playing with a tattered deck Noona had dug up somewhere and there stood the Preacher, a cynical smile on his face.

"Probably cheating," he said.

Vent pulled an ace of clubs from the deck and carefully placed it above the columns of cards. "Know anybody who don't cheat at solitary?"

The Preacher came and sat down against the wall. "You planning on wintering here?"

"I could do worse," Vent said, then asked, "Watson?"

"Still hanging around town, mostly with Holliday and Earp."

"Angel Brown? She show up?"

"Nope. Nobody knows what happened to her, but her daddy's in the act and it seems he's got some damn big medicine. The governor's beginning to ask some questions and Behan's having a hard time answering them."

Vent thought about that, then said slowly, "I figure she's being hidden out at Alexander's mine or she's down some shaft somewhere."

"Could be. If them gents would go so far as to hang a bunch of innocent men, they ain't a reason in the world why they should hold back doing in a woman, especially if that feller Birch had something to do with it."

"He been around?"

"He's vanished too. Marshal from Benson came looking for him. Didn't find him."

Vent stared at him. "What the hell did he want Birch for?"

The Preacher looked grim as he said, "The man, if you can call him that, raped and beat hell outa a Injun girl that works for the stage line. Seems as how a lot of folks put considerable store by her."

Vent shook his head. "Reckon I'm gonna notch my gun on him," he said, and the Preacher looked into his eyes and looked away. Death crouched there, waiting for the right time and place, and the Preacher knew that if someone didn't get to Birch first, Vent would kill him.

Now Vent rose, drank deep from the water can and offered the dipper to the old gambler. "The Ringo Kid came to the cabin and asked after me. Had three hardcases with him. One of them was Rudy Timkins."

"Who's the Injun girl?" the Preacher asked.

"Name's Noona," Vent said. "Related to old Vitorio up in the Dragoons. Seems she's got herself a bad habit . . . She makes her living off men."

"Ummm . . . Oldest profession, huh. In some societies, she'd be honored," the Preacher mused.

"How'd you find me?" Vent asked curiously.

The Preacher grinned. "The soiled dove came and found me in Tombstone. Tolled me into an alley, and when I was about to tell her she was picking on the wrong gent, she spoke your name. I just sorta followed her back here."

Vent shook his head. "Damnedest thing I ever saw, the way these Injuns seem to know what's going on."

"They do have listening posts around, don't they?"

Noona came in, smiled at the Preacher and touched a lock of gray hair dangling from beneath the brim of his hat and said mischievously, "Old man has gray on his head, but Noona knows he has fire in his spirit," and she giggled.

Vent grinned. "Looks like you done won a heart," he observed, and, walking to the cave entrance, leaned against the rock and gazed toward the distant smoke trails marking the ore mills of Dragoon.

The Preacher ignored Vent's sally. "Can you travel?"

"I can travel, but I figure maybe it might be better if you and me sorta moved by night. No use letting these slickers know what we're about.''

"Hell, I don't even know what we're gonna do.''

"First, we're going to locate Angel, whether she's dead or alive. Then, we're going to start whittling away at Alexander's bunch.''

"What about Ringo?''

"He bulletproof or something?''

"No, but he's damn fast. . . .''

"Can he beat me?''

The Preacher shook his head. "They ain't nobody can beat you, that is unless they lay out behind a rock and put one between your shoulder blades.''

"They already tried that,'' Vent said ruefully, touching his side where a puckered scar indicated someone was shooting damn well considering they did their ambushing in the dark of night.

"Where do we start?''

Noona took Vent's arm and asked, "You going away now?''

He smiled at her. "For a while. I'll be back. Tell your brother we will meet again. I owe him a great debt and Leatherhand does not forget.''

"I will tell him,'' and then she looked at the Preacher. "Bring the old one back when you come. Noona will show him a trick.''

Angel Brown awoke to the sound of someone singing softly and, sitting up in bed, looked around the room vacantly for a long moment before she recalled how she had gotten here. After escaping the Alexander mine, she had made a wide swing around the base of a rise of low hills to the west of Tombstone, planning on riding up to the back of the San José House and asking the owner to send her boy to fetch Had Putnam or Vent Torrey if they were in town. Somehow, she did not believe they had been killed in the ambushes arranged by the mysterious colonel, even though he bragged about having killed them.

She had just turned the corner into Sixth when she saw Rudy Timkins and a dark-looking man stop their horses in the street and begin an animated conversation. Slowly backing the horse along the alley, she reached Safford Street and turned the horse down it, riding at a careful walk. Halfway between Sixth and Fifth streets, she came abreast of a squat adobe building and a woman's voice suddenly said quietly, "Maybe you best take that hoss around back and come inside, miss," and Angel pulled the horse up and peered toward a doorway but couldn't make out a face to go with the dark shape standing there.

"Who are you?" she asked.

"Just a fellow traveler along the trail of life." The woman chuckled.

"Why should I stop here?" Angel asked reasonably.

"Obviously you're trying to hide from someone and I reckon it's most likely a man. We women should stick together. The invitation still stands."

On a sudden hunch Angel decided to trust the woman, even though she couldn't see her face and didn't know who she was. "Where's your corral?" she asked.

"They's a small corral and a horse shed around there," and the woman stepped out into the street and the light shone down on her. Angel looked at her curiously and saw a tall, busty female with large eyes, full lips and a prowlike nose gazing up at her. "You gonna set there all night?"

Angel rode around behind the house and led the horse into the corral, where a big dark gelding nickered softly and came to investigate this newcomer. She checked to make sure the water tank abutting the fence was full, then went back into the shed, found a pitchfork and dug some hay from a stack behind a stall, dumped it in the corner of the corral and watched as her horse went eagerly to it.

"That looks like John Peal's horse," the woman said.

Deciding not to lie to this woman, Angel said, "Could be. I stole him tonight."

Laughing softly, the woman led Angel through a back door, closed it carefully and dropped a bar in place, then went to the front door and barred it in turn. There were no windows in the front wall and only one side window looking out to the south, and when the woman fired up a lamp, Angel saw it was covered with a heavy muslin curtain.

"My name's Kate," the woman said.

Angel looked at her, noted the low-cut blouse displaying a generous amount of bosom and the remnants of lip paint and guessed her hostess was probably employed in one of the saloons.

"You guessed it, lady, I'm a whore," the woman said, and Angel, somewhat taken aback, still found she wasn't shocked and realized she had done a lot of growing up in the last few weeks.

"Would you like some coffee?" Kate asked, and Angel nodded, then looked around at the interior of the adobe and saw that a door led to a bedroom where a rumpled bed hugged the wall. Angel wondered if the woman plied her trade here, then moving down the room toward the built-in fire box in one wall, where a coffeepot hung from a cross-iron over a blaze of mesquite sticks, she saw a clothes rack next to the bed and was surprised to note several expensive suits hanging there, with half a dozen pairs of boots sitting in a row below them.

Seeing the direction of her gaze, Kate shrugged. "Oh, those belong to Doc. He sleeps here sometimes."

"Doc?" Angel asked.

"Ummm . . . Doc Holliday, the dentist . . . we . . . sorta got an arrangement. . . ."

Angel stared at her, then suddenly sat down. "My God, I could have rode all over Arizona and never hit on this," and when Kate raised an eyebrow Angel told her her story, sipping the rich coffee and munching on several biscuits as she talked.

When she finished, Kate said, "Honey, you need some rest. Me, I'll go fetch Doc and then we'll make us a plan," and she threw a shawl over her handsome shoulders and walked to the door. "Better stand away from the light and as soon as I leave you put the bar back in place. When we get back, we'll knock real loud, but don't you open the door until you ask who's there."

Angel followed her instructions, then went to the bed and, staring down at it, conjured up a picture in her mind of the robust Kate plying her trade here with some miner. As a flush crept up her body, she shook her head, lay down and was almost immediately asleep.

When she awoke it was to the sound of knocking on the front door. At the door she stood and waited until the knock came again.

"Miss Brown, it's me, Kate," a voice called, and Angel removed the bar and stepped clear of the door as Kate entered the room, followed by the slight blond figure of the famous gunfighter.

He removed his hat and bowed. "Miss Brown, I'm happy to find you alive and apparently in good health."

Going to the fire, she sat down in a chair and said, "It wasn't because those men who took me wanted it that way."

"Colonel Alex and his men kidnap you?" Holliday's voice was cold.

"Yes, he and a man he called Rudy and Baldy Birch, the robber who held up the Prescott stage and got away with my daddy's money."

"That Birch is a bad one." Holliday nodded.

Angel looked away. "Not anymore he isn't. I shoved him down a mine shaft when he tried to attack me. He fell all the way to the bottom and it sounded as if that hole was a mile deep."

Holliday stared at her. "You shoved Birch into a mine shaft? Well I'll be damned," and he looked around at Kate and said: "That'll save the price of some good hemp."

"She pried some boards off the back of the room they had her in and sneaked off," Kate volunteered.

Holliday went into the bedroom and returned with a full bottle of whiskey and two glasses. Glancing at Angel, he said, "You'll pardon us if we have a drink in front of you, Miss Brown?"

"Of course," Angel said, then a gleam came into her eye as she added, "I'd appreciate a small one myself."

Grinning, Holliday fetched a third glass, then toasted both women. "To two of the loveliest ladies in Cochise County," he said, and tossed off the drink.

Kate and Angel followed suit and Angel, who occasionally joined her father in a drink, felt the fire of the hot liquor and longed to return to the bed.

Glancing at her, Kate said, "I think our guest needs to go back to bed, Doc. She looks worn-out."

Angel smiled. "What's happened since they took me?"

Holliday looked at Kate, then cleared his throat. "We went looking for you. Vent got hit and I'm sorry to be the one to tell you this, but Had Putnam's dead. They killed him in the ambush they laid for us."

She felt the tears will up behind her eyes and threaten to spill over. She had known Had Putnam since she was a small girl and had always respected him. Now he was dead, trying to rescue her. And that quiet man, Vent Torrey, was wounded. "How bad was Mr. Torrey hurt?"

"Got hit in the side." Holliday told her of the events that had occurred near the Alex mine.

"You mean, Vent has disappeared?" she asked in wonder, thinking maybe he was lying out there somewhere helpless.

"Just seemed to vanish," Holliday said. "Wyatt and the Preacher rode all over hell looking for him. Nothing."

"Where would he go?"

"If he ain't dead, he may be holed up somewhere near Dragoon or Benson, or he might have rode into the Dragoons."

Kate drew in a long breath. "Let's hope he didn't go there. Them damned Apache'll lift his hair for sure."

"He could still handle a gun," Holliday said.

Nodding at Angel, Kate asked, "What about her?"

Holliday grinned. "Let's just keep her under wraps for a while," and turned to Angel. "That suit you?"

"It's probably better than giving that colonel another chance at me," she said ruefully.

Holliday left the two women and made his way to the Oriental, where he found Wyatt Earp in a poker game. Sliding into a chair near the back of the room, Holliday raised his head a fraction and waited while Earp counted his chips and announced he was sitting out a couple of hands and came to where Holliday sat and said, "Outside?"

Nodding, Holliday rose and led the marshal out. "The Brown woman came in. She's at Kate's."

"She all right?"

"Yes, but if Baldy Birch had gotten his way, she would have lost her innocence for sure," Holliday said, and his voice held winter winds.

"Damned rapist," Earp snapped.

"He's raped and beat his last woman," Holliday said with satisfaction. "Seems he tried to attack the Brown woman in one of the shaft houses and she hauled off and lambasted him with a hammer and knocked him off into a shaft about a mile deep. The bastard fell all the way to the bottom, she said."

Earp chuckled softly. "Couldn't have happened to a more deserving man."

"I told Kate to keep her hidden at the house until we figure out how we can use this," Holliday said.

"Well, I'm beginning to wonder if Behan and his boys are hooked onto this plow," Earp mused. " 'Pears to me like maybe this here Alex feller's on a high old lonesome all his own."

"Well, if the Clantons and the McLaurys ain't in it, you can bet they will be," Holliday said.

"By the way, the Mexicans got Old Man Clanton and Jim Crane down along the border two days ago."

Holliday whistled softly. "So, now it's Ike, Phin and Billy."

"Hear anything more about Torrey?" Earp watched a man walk along the opposite side of the street. "That looks like Hugo Richards."

Holliday turned and had his look. "Mr. *Tombstone Nugget*," he grunted, and watched the newspaper man turn along Fremont and guessed he was going to the livery stable he and Behan owned in partnership.

"Hell of a note," Earp said. "A crooked sheriff and a bent newspaper owner. Damned dangerous combination."

"Easy way to solve that. I'll just call Richards out. Hell, he's always writing editorials about me, calling me riffraff and such. Why not just weight him down with lead?"

"Not good," Earp said. "You do that and Behan will hang you for sure."

"Well, I could just sort of make sure old Johnny was there too, and then after I plugged Richards, let fly and miss and bore Behan through the brisket all accidental-like," Holliday mused idly, a grin on his face.

Earp stared at him, then said, "Sometimes, Doc, you scare the hell outa me. Let's go get a drink."

Colonel William J. Alex, owner of the Diamond-D Silver and Cattle Company, was worried. One of his men had returned from Tombstone with word that Angel Brown's father was requesting the governor of the territory to send troops from Fort Hauchuca to search Cochise County for his daughter.

Alex could not afford to have troops fooling around in the area, maybe digging up things out of the past better left buried.

These days he seldom ever thought about the Bandera Massacre, but now he deliberately allowed his mind to move back in time and thought about those eight men and how Smackler and the others pulled them up one at a time and strangled them. They should have hanged the Watson kid too, he thought, knowing that someday soon he must kill the rancher or lose in the end. He hadn't expected Jim Watson to turn out to be as hard a man as he now appeared to be. And to discover the man's uncle was none other than the Preacher, who had gunfighting friends all over the west, including Vent Torrey, rated as even better than Holliday, Earp or Bill Hickok, was a shock. In the beginning all he had set out to do was blackmail Watson for enough money to get his mine and cattle company back on its feet. With the bank about to take over everything, lock, stock and mine shafts, he had to do something. Over the years he had kept track of Jim Watson because somehow he regarded him as a silent threat loose out there who might come back to haunt him. It was Major William Alexander's, a.k.a Colonel William Alex, way of covering his back trail. Watson was the one witness outside the circle who could point to him as the man who stood by and let his men hang eight innocent travelers. On the other hand, Alexander hoped he had enough on Watson to keep him in line.

Thinking about Birch and how they had discovered his body at the bottom of the mine shaft and the girl gone, Alexander didn't have to twist his mind around too much to know what had happened. He was relieved to be rid of the man and soon he knew he'd have to put Timkins down the same shaft and then cave it in. Contreas was another matter. Alexander didn't delude himself into thinking the Mexican would be easily trapped. The man was as dangerous as a rattler and just as merciless.

The door opening interrupted his reverie and he turned and nodded and said, "Jim, what's happening in Tombstone?"

Watson grinned and, reaching into a pocket of his cougarskin vest, withdrew a tobacco sack and carefully rolled a cigarette. "They's another way we can do this, Major."

Alexander looked at him closely. Watson's face gave away nothing. "How's that?"

"We can quit trying to blackmail each other and join forces."

"To what end?" Alexander asked curiously.

Watson grinned toughly and pulled on his cigarette. "They's a lot of money to be made here. You and me, we could take over the cattle business out of Mexico and make a pile."

Alexander stared at him. "Hell, man, you already own half of Texas. What the hell do you want with more?"

Watson looked at the floor. "I want every damn thing I can get. I want my ranch to become as big as the King Ranch or John Slaughter's spread."

Alexander shook his head. "No wonder you fought so hard against me blackmailing you. You just ain't about to give up one damn thin buffalo, now are you?"

"Nope, not one thin buffalo," Watson agreed.

Alexander glanced toward the door. "Ringo's just outside there. Suppose I call him in and have him punch your ticket. What then?"

"I might just fool you, Major. I ain't no slouch with a handgun and one damn thing you can take to the bank. I'll put a couple in you before the Kid ever gets in here."

Alexander laughed. "Mister, you sure are one raspy gent."

"I don't cotton to that kinda talk, Major. Man says things like that he's telling me what he'd like to do, only he ain't got the sand to bring it off."

Alexander suddenly stopped smiling. "Don't ever underestimate me, Jim. It might just cost you your life."

Watson was not intimidated. "If I go out, you'll hold my hand on the road to hell," he promised.

Chapter 8

Vent and the Preacher sat their horses on a low hill just west of the cluster of buildings that marked the headquarters of the Diamond-D Silver and Cattle Company. They had arrived half an hour before dawn and now Vent stepped down from his horse and glancing around, led him out of sight of the mine. A huge pile of boulders, deposited there by some forgotten glacier, made the perfect hiding place. As he moved down a narrow pathway to the center of the natural corral, the Preacher came in behind him, still on horseback, dismounted, looked around and grunted, "Nice place to get boxed."

Vent had to agree, but still it was better than leaving the animals where any passing Alexander rider might accidentally spot them.

Squatting, they shared Vent's canteen and a loaf of Indian bread Noona had given them, then the Preacher rose and went to his saddlebags and returned with an old newspaper wrapped around several large chunks of well-cooked beef.

Handing a slice to Vent, he said, "Got these from the

restaurant at the Oriental. Figured they probably came from stolen Mexican beef . . . by the way, heard them greasers downed Old Man Clanton somewhere along the border.''

Vent looked up. ''Hell, Earp had him figured for that bullion train massacre down there. Mexicans probably decided to even the score.''

''They say he walked away from that one with over two million dollars,'' the Preacher said.

Vent shook his head. ''If he did, he must of buried her. He and them boys of his sure as hell didn't live like they had two million.'' He raised the canteen and chased the last of the meat down his throat with the sweet spring water from above Noona's cabin and jerked his head up slope. ''Reckon we better find a hidey-hole,'' and led the way to the top of the hill, leaving the horses ground-tied where they were.

Squatting behind a screen of bushes, the two men watched the sun rise and send its revealing light down upon the sprawl of buildings below, then Jim Watson left the mine office and walked around the building, returned aboard the grulla he favored and, stopping in front of the building as a man came to the door, pushed his hat back and spoke to him. Watson then whirled the horse and took the road to Tombstone.

''What the hell you make of that?'' Vent asked.

''Damn whelp's either sold out or he's been using us all along,'' the Preacher grunted, and looking at him, Vent wondered if the old man had enough hard bark on him to down his own blood kin and decided he probably did.

''What I can't figure is why he's doing it.'' Vent stared vacantly at the mining layout five hundred feet down slope from them.

''We know damn well Jim wanted most of them boys dead because of the way he went after Smackler and the two gunsels we killed in Shakespeare, but why let Alexander off the hook if the man sent him to Fredericksburg?'' the Preacher wondered.

"Hell, Alexander knows who he is. He's never tried to hide his identity.''

The Preacher turned and stared at Vent, then said, "Maybe he never was in Fredericksburg. . . .''

Vent sat back on his haunches and thought about it for a long moment, then said, "Preacher, when we leave here, maybe you best slip into town and ask Earp to wire the federals and have them check the records and see if Watson went to that prison. If we're lucky we may find out he was never there. . . .''

"And if that's so, then he must have made a deal somewhere on the road north from the Bandera hills,'' the Preacher mused.

"What kind of a deal is the puzzle,'' Vent said. "It had to be between him and Alexander and it had to be something that the others knew, and because they knew they were a threat to Jim. . . .''

Looking at the Missourian, the Preacher observed, "Sometimes you worry me, Mr. Torrey, the way your brain works. It's downright frightening.''

"You been doing some fancy figuring your ownself.'' Vent chuckled, then, looking down toward the mine, added, "That feller with the light hat, that's the Ringo Kid.''

The Preacher peered through the branches of their hiding place. "My, ain't he a dandy?''

"Yep, shore is. Feller's almost pretty. Got wavy hair and a fancy little mustache and wears six months' wages on his back.''

"Hear he's a gent born with more than his share of hot pepper in his veins,'' the Preacher observed.

Vent nodded. "They say when that boy loses his temper every man looks the same size to him.''

"Well, him and Doc would make a good pair."

They lazed through the day watching the Diamond-D mine and Vent, still a bit weak from his wound, dozed off and on while the Preacher played lookout. Vent was asleep when darkness finally claimed the land and then the Preacher touched him lightly on the shoulder and the tall gunfighter was immediately awake and alert. "Time to move."

Vent rose stiffly and led the way back over the hill. They didn't return directly to their horses, but instead moved to the opposite side of the pile of boulders, and while the Preacher stood near a narrow aperture leading to the hidden corral, Vent carefully climbed to the top of a boulder and peered down. The horses stood patiently waiting, obviously undisturbed by their surroundings.

Half an hour later, they rode into the outskirts of Tombstone, where Vent slipped into an alley and watched as the Preacher's tall frame disappeared toward the OK Corral.

As he stood leaning against the wall of an adobe house at the end of Fremont Street, a rider came along and, passing beneath a street lamp, gave off fire from enough silver trimming on his clothes to start a bank with. Watching the man, Vent waited. Somehow, he knew the rider had seen him there and was watching him from the corner of his eye.

Deliberately, Vent rolled a cigarette, removed a match from his hatband and lit up, watching the rider over his fists.

Turning his horse, the man rode to a spot directly opposite Vent and asked, *"Quien es?"* and Vent knew this wasn't a white man speaking Mexican, but a Mexican speaking his own language.

"Nadie," Vent answered.

Apparently detecting the English inflection in the words,

the rider now spoke the same language. "There's no such person as nobody, hombre. Everybody's somebody."

"*No yo,*" Vent said softly, still speaking Mexican.

"*Que hace usted?*" the rider suddenly snapped, and the horse shifted its position, giving Vent a quick glimpse of a badge. Contreas, he thought, and let his hand drop to his belt just above his gunbutt.

"*Tenga cuidado,*" the deputy warned him, and Vent thought, Be careful yourself, and replied, "*No tengo nada,*" and flipped the tiedown from his gun hammer, the darkness hiding his movements.

"I'm always careful"—he spoke in English and deliberately kept his voice low—"el Jefe. . . ."

The Mexican knew he was at a disadvantage. He was sitting on his horse in the light of the street lamp while this stranger lurked in the darkness of an alley. "*Que hace usted?*" he repeated.

"Waiting for a girl," Vent said softly, and laughed in his throat.

"Ahhh . . . *Comprendo,*" and gigging his horse, the deputy rode on and Vent thought, I'll bet you have a bad itch between your shoulder blades, friend Contreas, and watched him out of sight.

As the Mexican deputy turned in at the livery jointly owned by John Dunbar and Johnny Behan, a soft laugh came from the alley. The Preacher led his horse up to where Vent waited and, looking after Contreas, asked, "What was that all about?"

"Fancy dude got just a bit too nosy. Thought I'd play a little game with him. Reckon he lost."

"Damn fool bracing a man while sitting out there in the middle of the street on a big old white horse, and you back here in this alley," the Preacher observed.

"Won't live long, he keeps that up," Vent agreed. "You find Earp?"

"He's sending the wire. Said we should have an answer by tomorrow night if we get lucky."

Vent looked toward the lights of Allen Street. "Me, I could eat the south end of a cow going north. Why don't we just sashay on over and find us a place to put on the feed bag?"

The Preacher grinned. "Not a bad idea."

When they reached Allen, he kept to the middle of the street to avoid the sidewalk crowd, walked along in the shadow of his horse. Vent followed suit.

When they reached a small café halfway between Fifth and Fourth streets, the Preacher tied the stud to the hitchrack and Vent, noticing a water trough fifty feet down the street, said, "Wait," and went and let the Appaloosa dip his nose in the cool water.

As the big horse drank his fill, Vent watched the street. The horse raised its head and blew water into the dust and Vent led him back to where the Preacher waited and the two entered the restaurant together, moving immediately to a table in the back of the room where the lamp cast long shadows up the wall. They ordered steak and eggs and a double portion of fried potatoes and the waiter went away and returned with the traditional huge coffeepot and two cups.

When the meal arrived, they dug in wordlessly, cleaning their plates in record time, then watched the waiter fill their cups with the hot black brew.

"Black enough to float a Winchester, but that's how I like it," the Preacher said.

Vent chuckled softly, and then a man came in the front door and said something to the waiter, who shook his head, and walked through a door in the rear of the counter.

"Now what?" Vent wondered softly, watching the newcomer, who wore a brace of .45s tied down to his leg in cavalry holsters he had cut the flaps off of and a huge Bowie knife in a boot scabbard.

Turning, the man walked back to where Vent and the Preacher sat and, peering into the semidarkness, asked, "Either of you fellers own that Appaloosa out there?"

"Why?" Vent asked.

"So happens that there pony belongs to me," the man said. "Won him in a poker game up in Prescott a year ago. Somebody up and ran off with him three weeks back. I trailed him south."

"You're a damned liar," Vent said quietly.

"What?" the man growled, and stepped back, his hands dropping to his guns.

Vent stared at him. "What kinda sandy you trying to run, feller?"

"No damn sandy. That's my horse. You come on out there and I'll show you how I can prove it."

So that's the game, Vent thought, and suddenly magicked the .44 into his hand and said, "Mister, I think you're part of a setup, and if you are, you're history."

Hastily moving his hands wide of his body, the two-gun man said, "Now wait, feller. No need for that. Maybe I made a mistake."

The Preacher rose and said quietly, "You may have made your last mistake. Who put you up to this game?"

Looking over his shoulder as if expecting help from that quarter, the man suddenly said, "To hell with it. Me, I ain't gonna get kilt over something that brought me a silver dollar. They's half a dozen men out there staked on your horses. They sent me in to toll you out. They said you was outlaws."

"What's your name?" Vent asked coldly.

"Dee Hargrove, from Missouri," the man said, and swallowed nervously.

"My name's Torrey, Mr. Hargrove. You know me?"

The man swallowed and said shakily, "Hell, yes, Mr. Torrey. Everybody in Missouri has heard of you and them Hawkses."

Nodding his head toward the old gambler, Vent said, "This here's the Preacher. You know him?"

"Of course," Hargrove said, and then added, "And me, I'm the damn fool who came in here to toll you boys outside. Hell, I didn't know what was happening here."

"The back door is right over there," Vent said. "You just drift on out and I reckon if you've got a home you best head for it."

Staring at Vent as if he had just received a reprieve, Hargrove drew a deep breath. "Me, I feel like the gent who was on his way to the gallows and told the preacher, 'This here'll sure teach me a lesson,' " and Vent, liking the man's ability to joke in the face of the possibility he might be dead in another three seconds, said, "You'll walk out that door without a worry, Mr. Hargrove. We don't back-shoot. If I wanted you dead, I'd kill you where you stand," and holstered his .44 and waited.

"I reckon I owe you one, Mr. Torrey. I'll not forget," and Vent answered, "I reckon you do," and watched him leave.

The Preacher sat back down and picking up his coffee cup, took a swallow and made a face. "The damn stuff is cold."

Vent picked up his cup and gazed at the door over the rim. "We wait too long and they're gonna figure they been burned."

The tall old gambler rose and, pulling back his coattails, adjusted the hang of his .45s, lifting away the hammer tiedowns in the process, and half grinning, said, "Let's us kinda drift out after old Hargrove, then take a stroll along the alley and peek around the corner. Who knows what we might find waiting." He led the way to the back door where he found the restaurant owner staring at them wide-eyed.

"Something wrong, neighbor?" Vent asked as he dug out a silver dollar and paid him for the food.

The man cleared his throat. "I couldn't help overhearing what you fellers was talking about. You ain't gonna go out there, are ya?"

Vent shrugged. "Hell, man, we can't hunker down in here the rest of our lives."

Looking the kitchen over, the Preacher, a twinkle in his eyes, observed, "Might not be a bad idea. Seems this here gent's got plenty of grub on hand."

Vent shook his head. "Wouldn't work. They'd just come in after us and probably plug this poor feller for hiding us," and the restaurant owner swallowed, tried on a grin for size and found it didn't quite fit.

Slapping him on the shoulder, Vent said, "Needn't worry, pard. We're gonna take this to the street. Hell, with all the shooting going on in this town, they ain't nobody who'll miss a swallow of his drink when the shebang begins," and ducked through the back door and ran lightly along the alley until he reached a narrow walkway between the buildings. Stopping, he held up his hand and then waved the Preacher forward and pointed toward Allen Street, where a dark shadow crouched, peering around the corner.

Then the waiting ambusher moved and a streetlight caught the sheen of a sawed-off shotgun and Vent stepped into the opening and said, just loud enough so the man could hear him, "Waiting for somebody?"

With a curse, the shotgunner whirled and whipped up his weapon. Coldly, Vent slammed a bullet into his chest as the shotgun went off with a thunderous roar straight up, ripping a huge hole in the restaurant's porch roof. The terrible blow of Vent's .44 slug hurled the man across the sidewalk and into the street, where he fell heavily, drew up his knees and then kicked once and died.

A wild curse greeted this action as Vent and the Preacher ducked back from the walkway and raced north, ducking down a similar alleyway alongside a shoe shop. Bursting into Allen, Vent lifted his gun and fired at a crouched figure in the process of swinging up a pistol and watched him collapse with a scream. A bullet ripped the wood from the corner of the building and Vent heard the Preacher curse and called, "Hit?" and was answered by more cursing.

Figuring anybody who could cuss like that had to be all right, the Missourian ran straight out into Allen, catching two gunmen flat-footed just as they leaped clear of the alley where the shotgunner had been hiding.

The Preacher, crouched over his twin .45s, hosed a stream of lead into them and, not waiting to see if he scored, wheeled and shot a man loose from behind a porch support across Allen. As the man stumbled away from the post, his spurs became entangled and he pitched off the sidewalk, screaming, "Ah . . . God, I'm hit. . . ." and tumbled into the dust.

Vent stood boldly upright in the middle of the street and traded shots with a man he had recognized as Rudy Timkins and was rewarded when one of his bullets tagged the escaped murderer, spinning him around and driving him into the building behind him. He hung there for a long moment, then slid down the wall to the sidewalk, dropping his pistol.

Marking him finished, Vent whirled at the sound of a running horse and found himself directly in the path of a big bay stud racing full out, the rider on its back leaning far over with outthrust pistol spurting pencils of flame.

"Look out, Preacher!" Vent shouted, and, dodging to the left, lifted his .44 and pulled the trigger, only to discover he had fired his last shot. Diving behind a water trough, he punched out the empties and quickly reloaded, watching the street as he did, then the Preacher gave a wild Rebel yell and, dropping to one knee, fired straight up into the rider's face. The bullet entered just below his chin and literally heaved him up and over the cantleboard to slam facedown in the dust as the horse dodged the crouching gambler and ran full tilt into the window of the restaurant, showering a running gunman with shards of glass. Vent rose and pounded off a shot and saw the man's legs become entangled as he seemed to run forward in a leaning position that became more and more pronounced until he hit flat on the sidewalk and skidded off into the gutter.

He saw the Preacher, his coattails flying, two .45s fisted in gnarled hands, running south as three men came dashing from an alley to head him off. It was a fatal mistake. The old gunfighter suddenly slid to a stop and his guns spoke a rolling song of death as he cut them down.

Vent ran to the horses and, jerking the reins loose, leaped on the back of the Appaloosa and, leading the Preacher's stud, raced to where he stood punching out empties.

"Coming up behind you," Vent shouted, and the Preacher turned, slammed his weapons into leather and grabbed the saddle horn as Vent whirled past, and then he was into the leather and they rounded off Allen Street as a bullet ripped a hole in a dangling sign, knocking it loose from its chains. As it fell, Vent turned, lifted his .44 and fired once. A man just rounding the corner with a rifle clutched in his hands stopped suddenly as if he had struck an adobe wall, then pitched into the dirt and lay dead, an unmoving shadow along the ground.

The sudden roar of gunfire on Allen Street galvanized Wyatt and Virgil Earp and Doc Holliday into instant action as Earp snapped, "That's no drunken cowboy," and ran for the door.

Two blocks along the street, the marshal and chief of police saw lancing flame bite the dark, and Holliday said, "They's one hell of a gunfight going on down there," and then a stray slug smashed a window behind them and all three dropped as if shot.

Looking along the sidewalk, Earp made a decision. "Better wait it out. We don't know who the hell those fellers are. Might get on the wrong side," and so they lay and waited as guns tore at each other and the solid thunk of slugs striking buildings heralded near misses.

Then Johnny Behan came dodging along the front of the buildings and dropped beside Wyatt and asked breathlessly, "What in tarnation's going on down there?"

"Damned if I know," Wyatt replied. "Sounds like some fellers got one hell of a difference of opinion going," then his voice was drowned out as a pair of .45s opened up.

"Whoever's handling them forty-fives knows what the hell he's about," Holliday observed.

"By God, that's a damned outrage," Behan shouted as a bullet struck a hitching post two feet from his head.

"You better keep your bean down, Johnny, or somebody down there's gonna blow it off," Virgil advised as another slug slammed into a window somewhere.

As Behan started to answer, they heard a horse scream, then a window collapsed and a man cried out in awful agony.

"Who is it?" Clum, the newspaperman, asked. He had come up behind the prone men on hands and knees and now lay beside Earp.

"Damned if I know, John," Wyatt replied.

"My God, they're slaughtering each other," Behan said,

then looking accusingly at Virgil, added: "Dammit, Virgil, you're the chief of police. Do something."

"What the hell do you suggest?" Virgil asked reasonably as the firing suddenly stopped and was replaced by the sound of running horses.

As Behan started to answer, a lone shot was fired from a rifle and answered by a pistol. From where the men lay, they could see a man suddenly stop running near an intersection two blocks south and then drop facedown in the middle of the street.

"Done, by God," Holliday said, and rose to his feet.

The little group of lawmen rose and, followed by the newsman, walked cautiously forward until they reached the edge of the battleground. Looking around at the carnage, Behan shook his head.

"Whoever them fellers was, they sure tore the hell outa this town," he observed, then turning, saw that a large crowd was gathering and shouted: "Go on about your business. This here's law stuff," and was promptly ignored.

Holliday knelt beside a man and rolled him over, then looked up at Earp and said quietly, "One of Alex's men. Now what the hell do you make of that?"

Virgil called from down street, his voice husky. "These fellers is all dead. Plugged through and through."

As Behan and Virgil Earp prowled among the dead, Wyatt and Holliday moved down a side street, and stopping against a building, Earp said, "I smell Leatherhand's gunwork in this mess."

"Him and old Preacher," Holliday agreed. "Hell, they isn't anybody in this town, including Johnny Ringo, that could do that kind of damage and ride away in one piece."

As they stood talking, Contreas came along the street on his big white horse and, seeing them there, reined the animal over as Holliday observed dryly, "That fancy horse and all that shiny junk's bound to get you plugged someday, Anselamo.''

The Mexican's teeth were a bright flicker in the night as he answered, ''A man who rides a white horse ain't no cow thief, amigo.''

Earp looked at him sourly and said, ''Man wearing a badge don't have to steal cattle, Mr. Contreas. Me, I been around law work too long not to know where the money lies if you're a mind to pick it up.''

The Mexican stopped smiling and nodded toward Allen Street. ''What happened out there?''

''Looks like somebody tried to take a bite outa a couple of catamounts and came away with their butt clawed,'' Earp said.

''Sounded like the Civil War being fought all over.'' Contreas shook his head and rode on toward Allen Street.

Watching him ride away, Holliday observed, ''Someday, Mr. Marshal, you're gonna ruffle that gent's feathers in the wrong direction and he's gonna go to the gun with you.''

''More like he'll lay out in an alley and back-shoot me,'' Earp said, and led the way back to Allen Street, where the mortician was loading bodies in his wagon with the help of several townsmen. Looking up at Earp, he said, ''Damn place looks like a slaughterhouse. Blood all over hell . . .''

''You shoot a man and he leaks,'' Holliday told him, and went to the wagon and had his look at the bodies. ''They's ten dead men in here.''

Virgil came over and stared at them, then shook his head. ''Now who the hell were those fellers?''

A man pushed his way through the crowd, came up to Virgil and, getting his attention, said, ''I caught a quick glimpse of them. They was only two men, Mr. Earp, and they rode down Fourth Street.''

"You get a look at their faces?" Virgil asked.

The man shook his head. "Too damn dark out here. Somebody shot out the streetlights when the fandango first opened up. All I saw was streaks of flame comin' from them damn guns. Me, I found a hole and got in it."

Virgil grinned. "Can't say as I blame you."

Behan was standing by the mortician's wagon and now he looked around at Holliday and called, "Doc, come over here for a minute, will you?"

The dentist strolled over, glanced at the bullet-gouged corpses and observed, "See how a man can wind up if he gets in over his head?"

"What the hell's that supposed to mean?"

Holliday grinned. "Just an observation, Mr. Sheriff."

Pointing at the bodies, Behan said accusingly, "These men all ride for Colonel Alex, out at the Diamond-D."

"So?"

"Well, dammit to hell, what they doing shooting up the town?"

Holliday shook his head. "It don't appear to me as if they did much more than wind up dead."

Virgil came over leading a horse and Holliday noticed it was limping badly. "Got the Diamond-D brand on its hip," Virgil said, then shaking his head, added: "Poor brute's got an awful bad glass cut on his ankle. Must of been the horse we heard fall through the window."

Holliday bent and lifted the injured leg. "Be better to put the poor damn brute away."

Behan also examined the animal, then searched the crowd until he spotted the blacksmith. "Hey, Abe, come have a look at this animal, will you," and stepped back as the heavy-shouldered blacksmith carefully examined the wound. Dropping the hoof, he shook his head and said, "I can try, but he'll probably have a damn weak leg. That's a hell of a cut."

Earp grunted, "I don't like seeing a horse killed. Take him down to the livery and do what you can, will you, Abe?"

As the blacksmith led the limping horse away, Behan turned and called out, "I want six men to ride to the Diamond-D with me. Who's it gonna be?"

Hank Swilling, a half-breed Pima Indian, stepped forward, followed by Pete Spence, Frank Patterson, a man known locally as Rattlesnake Bill, another Indian called Pony Deal and Joe Hill.

Wyatt glanced at Holliday and said softly, "All the damn outlaws in the country."

"Hell, maybe they'll get ambushed and wind up like poor old Bratton . . . all shot to hell." Holliday grinned.

Behan, who was standing ten feet away and clearly heard him, turned and said harshly, "Maybe you outa come along, Doc. The night air'll do you good."

Holliday shook his head. "Why thanks, Mr. Behan, but seems to me if I did that, I'd stand a good chance of some trigger-happy feller letting some of that night air into my head through the back rather than getting much of a chance to breath it in through the front."

"What the hell's that supposed to mean?" Pete Spence, who fancied himself quite a gunman, snapped, glaring at Holliday.

Voice suddenly cold and desolate, Holliday stared at him from his expressionless gray eyes and said softly, "It means, you son of a bitch, that if you open your mouth again, I'm going to play dentist, only I won't pull your teeth. I'll blow them out," and his hand dropped to the butt of one of his .45s as he waited, muscles tensed.

Earp and his brother ranged alongside Holliday and waited, then Holliday said, "Your move, Mr. Behan."

Suddenly Ike Clanton swaggered around the corner of Fourth, stopped and stared at the confrontation, then began slowly drawing his weapon. He had it almost clear of leather and still hadn't been observed when a cold voice followed by the colder click of a pistol being put on full cock, said, "Better keep that in leather, Mr. Clanton, or I'm gonna bend your backbone."

Glancing over his shoulder, Clanton looked into the quiet eyes of Morgan Earp and said viciously, "Either shoot that thing or get away from me."

Without a word, Morgan lifted the gun and brought it down savagely on Clanton's head, driving him to his knees. Reaching down, he collared him. "You're going to jail, you bastard, and if you resist anymore, I'm going to kill you," and pulling Clanton's gun from its holster, he began dragging him along the street toward city hall as the floundering cowboy cursed and struggled.

Back on the street, Behan had decided he wasn't ready for a showdown with the Earp faction quite yet and led his posse toward the livery without uttering a word. As he passed the corner, Curly Bill Brocius Graham, the man who had shot and killed former town marshal Fred White, stepped from the crowd and silently joined the posse.

Watching them go, Earp observed, "Looks like those fellers are out looking for trouble and if they go pushing around the Diamond-D, they may just get it."

Two miles west of town, Vent and the Preacher had stopped to allow their horses to blow and now they sat and looked back toward the glitter of lights that was Tombstone and said nothing. Vent wondered vaguely how they had managed to escape the fracas untouched, but marked it up to the kind of luck that, when reversed, saw a man drop on the first shot.

"Where to now, Mr. Torrey?" the Preacher asked.

"I think maybe Johnny Behan's gonna mount a posse and take in after us. He ain't gonna worry about Colonel

Alexander, even though he probably knows by now them was Alexander's boys we downed.''

The Preacher nodded in agreement, then realizing Vent couldn't see him in the dark, said, ''Reckon you're right. Time to hunt us a hole.''

''We could go back and stay in Noona's cave,'' Vent said. ''She seemed to take a liking to you, Preacher. Should make things pretty easy for us.''

The Preacher only grunted as the first distant sound of running horses leaving Tombstone came to them. Wheeling the Appaloosa, Vent led off to the west and all that night they rode steadily until just before daylight Vent called a halt and stepped down among a tangle of brush and boulders.

Rudy Timkins lay full length among the crumpled remains of an old building just off Allen and Fourth. He could hear the restless stamp of horses' hooves coming from somewhere and then somebody began cursing, and raising his head, he saw a man dragging another man along the street toward Fremont and wondered if one of Alexander's boys had got caught, then thinking back over the fight, decided it was probably something else unrelated to the recent disaster on Allen.

His head ached terribly and he wondered if he had been shot through it. Lifting a trembling hand, he carefully probed along a deep furrow above his left eyebrow and realized that he was alive only because by some fluke, he must have lifted his chin just as Torrey fired, thus avoiding catching the big .44 slug directly in the forehead. Thinking about it, he began to shiver and knew then he had to get away from town and get help.

Rising to his knees, he looked toward Allen and was in time to see a group of horsemen, led by Johnny Behan, ride north and figured they were on their way to Alexander's mine. Grinning painfully, he thought about Johnny Ringo and that gunsel Jim Watson waiting there and wondered who'd end up winning that game. He couldn't figure out what the hell Watson was playing for. He knew the man was out to kill every member of the troop that hanged his friends, yet he seemed to have no quarrel with Alexander. It didn't make sense. Smackler, Birch, Pete Jolly, Malone and Buel Courtney were all dead, as was the rest of the troop involved in the hanging. The only ones left now, Timkins realized, were he, Alexander and the deputy, Contreas.

"Contreas," he whispered, and knew that if he could find the man, he'd have his help. It was relatively quiet over on Allen Street now, quiet enough so Timkins felt he could chance standing up. On his feet, he discovered he was very weak and was forced to brace himself against an adobe wall in order to make it to Fourth. He still had a blistering headache and figured he probably had some kind of concussion up there. Turning onto Fremont, he hurried past city hall and then he was beneath the streetlight in front of the OK Corral. Moving on, he came to a white picket fence and was halfway past the house behind it when a cold voice said, "Stand pat, neighbor, or I'm just naturally gonna sift you through that picket fence."

Timkins stood perfectly still as he heard the sound of spurs jingling behind him, and with his breath choking him, he used every ounce of his willpower to remain where he was.

The man had stopped behind him and now he felt his gun being removed from its holster and a voice said, "Turn around, amigo, and let's take a look at you."

Slowly Timkins turned and found himself staring into the grinning face of Anselamo Contreas. "Well, I'll be damned!" he exclaimed, and then reached out and grabbed the picket fence to keep from falling.

Staring at him, the Mexican deputy said, "Looks like you was stacking bobcats and the bottom one slipped."

"That damned Leatherhand. Him and his pard, the old Preacher, they blew us to hell tonight."

Contreas shook his head. "Hell, man, you should have known you were outgunned. Them boys cut their teeth on a six-gun. They been to a lot of wars and they're still around."

"Dammit, they ain't bulletproof," Timkins said sullenly. His head ached like the furies.

Contreas took Timkins by the arm. "Come on with me. I got a place just up the street. We can fix you up there."

As they neared the corner of Third, Morgan Earp stepped from a house and turned toward them. Contreas cursed under his breath, then said softly, "Don't say a damn word. Let me handle this."

Morgan came on, and then stopped, hand dropping to his gun. "That you, Contreas?"

"Sí, it's me," the Mexican answered, and moved forward until he came up to the assistant marshal.

Looking at Timkins, Morgan asked, "What hit him, a runaway mine wagon?"

"Nope, feller pistol-whipped the poor bastard down on Allen," Contreas said. "Lives down here with a friend. I'm trying to get him home so they can fix him up, maybe call the sawbones, if need be."

"Need any help?"

The Mexican shook his head. "No, but thanks, Mr. Earp," and he moved off, crossed Third and then glanced back and noted the tall shape of Morgan just swinging down Fourth toward Allen.

Reaching a squat adobe, he turned in through a narrow wooden gate, carefully fastened it and crossed a small courtyard and through another heavy door into an ornate front room where a black-haired Mexican girl sat before a small fire laid on the hearth of a fireplace built into the wall.

Contreas said something in Spanish to her and she left the room as he led Timkins to a chair and helped him sit down. Bringing a lamp, he made a careful examination of the wound and shook his head. "Damn close thing, that."

The girl came back carrying a panful of water and a box, which she deposited on the table. While Contreas watched, she carefully cleaned the wound, dabbed some salve on it, which made Timkins flinch, then wrapped a bandage around it and tied it off in the rear. Stepping back, she smiled and said in soft English, "Now he looks like a pirate."

"He is a pirate," Contreas grunted, and led Timkins to a small bedroom and helped him off with his boots and jacket and watched as the little gunman stretched out on his back and dropped off to sleep.

Back in the front room, the deputy walked to where the girl was standing, looking into the flames, and, taking her in his arms, kissed her long and fervently. "I've got to go out again, *amor*, but I'll be back in about two hours. I'll wake you."

Leaning back in his arms, she said with a smile in her eyes, "If you don't, *querido*, I shall creep into the poor wounded man's bed and attempt to console him."

He smiled in return, but it didn't reach his eyes. "You be careful of that one, *cara*, he's very dangerous. Like a snake, he gives no warning. You keep your *pistola* close by, *querida*, and if he bothers you, shoot him. *Comprende?*"

She nodded, very serious now, and then he kissed her again and quietly left the room. As soon as the door closed, the girl went to a drawer and removed a vicious little Colt .44 derringer and slipped it into her pocket. Then humming softly, she went back to the fire and, using a hook, removed a pot from over the flames and filled a bowl with beans, took several floury tortillas from a pan on the table and began slowly eating, chasing the meal with wine from a large bottle.

Behind the adobe Contreas was saddling a horse. This time he chose a dark-colored animal and saddled it with a plain rig. Throwing a long cloak over his shoulders and fastening it at the neck, he mounted, wrapped himself in the cloth and, pulling his hat low, rode into the street. He did not pass directly through the town, but swung wide, riding up Tombstone Gulch and then breaking due west toward the San Pedro River.

At Watervale, he reined sharply west around the northern side of Allis Hill and was careful to keep clear of Wilson's Camp, even though he was sure the place had long since wrapped up its sidewalks and gone off to bed. Two miles from the Boquillas Ranch, Contreas pulled in his horse near a small adobe building, stepped down and, swinging his cloak clear of his gunbutts, strode around the structure, leading his horse.

" 'Lo there, amigo," Jim Watson said as he stepped around the corner, only to discover himself staring down the bore of a .45.

Contreas sighed. "Old compañero, you tread where angels shiver with fear."

"Knowed you wouldn't shoot, Anselamo. Hell, you're too old a hand to let fly at the moon. What's been happening in Tombstone?"

Moving in against the wall of the adobe as a desert wind began to stir the brush, Contreas rolled a cigarette, handed the tobacco to Watson and said casually, "Hell of a gunfight in town. Seems a bunch of Alexander's boys rode in and tried to rub out Leatherhand and the old Preacher. Bad mistake . . ."

Staring at him, Watson cupped his hands around a match as it flared up to highlight the plains of his face. "Oh . . ."

"Sí, they got sent off to shovel coal in hell and Leatherhand and the Preacher got clean away."

"I told Alexander that was a stupid move," Watson said disgustedly. "Timkins go down too?"

"He was lucky. Got hit in the head."

"Well, that probably didn't do him any damage," Watson agreed, a small grin on his tough face.

"Left a crease along his thick skull," Contreas said. "He managed to sneak off and I found him. He's at my place with 'Cheta."

"Hope she can take care of herself," Watson said dryly. "I wouldn't trust that little weasel any more than I would have trusted Birch."

"Would have?" Contreas asked.

Watson pulled on the last of his smoke, mashed it out with a sharp-toed boot, sending a faint spur rattle into the night, and said, "That Brown gal, she up and shoved him down a mine shaft when he tried to rape her . . . served the bastard right."

"He left a hell of a trail coming down here," Contreas said. "Half the sheriffs in the Southwest are looking for him for mistreating women."

"He's gone now," Watson grunted as the wind picked up. Moving restlessly away from the building and looking keenly at Contreas, he asked, "What now?"

"Simple. You get rid of Alexander and take over the mine and I'll take old Rudy out for a long ride and see that he doesn't make it back."

"Just like that?"

"Just like that, amigo. Timkins can no longer talk and neither can Alexander. Behan will make sure the records show we paid hard cash for the mine. The stock is another matter. I've talked to a man who will move it north and sell for a good price."

"Clanton?" Watson asked.

"Sí, Clanton."

"What makes you think that damned whelp will come back and pay you your share?"

"If he doesn't, the man I send with him will kill him," Contreas said simply.

"Who you sending, Holliday?"

Contreas laughed. "Don't I wish," he said. "No, Ringo will ride along."

"What if they get together and ride off into the sunset?"

Contreas threw back his head and laughed. "Damn, Watson, you're the most suspicious man I ever met. We can only put so many checks on this thing. If it goes sour, then we lose. It's that simple."

Watson shook his head. "I don't like losing."

"Hell, Clanton'll come back. He's got a ranch here and he needs Johnny Behan. If he runs, Johnny will outlaw him and he knows it. And if Johnny outlaws Ike, he'll outlaw Phin and Billy."

Moving back to the shelter of the adobe, Watson looked at the sky and said, "Damned if I can figure how them boys dodged jail this long."

Contreas laughed. "Hell, man, you know out here the line between the good and the bad is just about as blurred as an Indian pony's pedigree."

"If I tag Alexander, it'll have to be while Ringo's gone," Watson said. "Me, I don't hanker to come up against that man. He's as fast as greased owl shit and I got me this feeling he just naturally don't like Texacans."

Grinning, Contreas observed, "Amigo, they ain't nobody like Texacans, including Texacans themselves."

"They like Mexicans even less," Watson reminded him, and rode off without looking back.

"Stupid gringo," Contreas said, thinking that when it was all over, he'd take great pleasure in putting six .45 slugs right square in the Texan's guts.

For his part, Watson rode two hundred yards, then said, "Damned pepper belly. First chance I get after Timkins and the major are salted away, I'm gonna drop that chili eater."

Timkins awoke to find the Mexican girl sitting beside the bed, staring at him. Looking up at her, he said, "You got any water around here," and watched her rise and leave the room. She returned with a tin cupful and watched him greedily gulp it down.

"Food?" he asked.

Again she went away and returned with a plate of beans sided by a dozen flour tortillas and a double portion of cooked green peppers. He carefully tasted the food, for Timkins was no stranger to Mexican grub, knowing their penchant for flavoring everything with enough hot peppers to scald the lining from a man's stomach. Surprisingly, the food was well seasoned but not too hot, so he went at it as if he were starving, ignoring the girl until the dish was bare.

"More," he said, pushing it toward her.

He ate the second helping a little slower then asked if she had any coffee. She did. He drank two cups of the hot brew and began feeling a great deal better. Throwing a leg over the edge of the bed, he noticed his boots had been removed. Pointing to his sockless feet, he looked at her and raised an eyebrow. Nodding, she went and returned with his stockings. She had washed and dried them, and Timkins, who was not the most fastidious man in the world and smart enough to realize it, suddenly wanted a bath and a change of clothes. He smelled.

In halting Spanish, for he had never really gotten comfortable with the language, he asked for water and soap. A smile flashed across the girl's face and then she went to the other room and returned carrying a tub. Placing it in the center of the room, she made several more trips for hot water, seemingly having access to an endless supply. When the tub was full, she dropped in a cake of soap, pointed at his clothes and snapped her fingers.

Hesitatingly at first, then seeing she didn't appear the least embarrassed, he shucked out of his clothing and soon stood in his long-handles. Again she snapped her fingers imperiously, and shrugging, Timkins said, "What the hell," and disrobed completely.

Looking him over critically as if she were examining a side of beef, she finally smiled and, shrugging, said, "*Esta bien,*" and, gathering his clothes, strolled from the room as Timkins watched her swaying rear and wondered why the hell white women couldn't act that way.

While he bathed, 'Cheta washed his clothes and left them to dry on the hearth, then returned to the bedroom, where she found the outlaw sitting on the edge of the bed, smoking a cigarette.

"*Dentro de poco.*" She smiled, then said in English, "Pretty soon."

"Thanks . . . gracias," Timkins said, and then suddenly self-conscious, pulled the blanket across his waist and looked away as she turned and left the room.

Half an hour later, she returned with his clothes and while she watched unabashed, he put them on, wondering why the hell he didn't just grab the Mexican bitch and throw her into bed. For some reason, her childlike demeanor threw him off. She was not playing the usual female games with him. She was completely natural, acting as if she stood around and watched men dress all the time. Hell, he thought, maybe she does. Maybe she's a damn nurse, or something, then he suddenly decided to find out what she would do if he did make a pass. Wearing only his long-handles, he reached out and took her by the arm, pulled her against him and kissed her. She did not resist, but then she didn't join in the festivities either.

Stepping away, she held up an admonishing finger, shook it at him and left the room before he could move.

"Damn," he said to the wall, and finished dressing.

When Contreas returned, he found Timkins and 'Cheta quietly playing cards before the fireplace and sipping from the neck of a wine bottle. Standing with hands on hips, the Mexican deputy surveyed the scene and then shook his head, noting Timkin's obviously clean clothes and fresh bandage. "Looks like my lady took good care of you, amigo."

Coming to Contreas, the girl put her arms around him and kissed him soundly, then said, "Mr. Teemkins' clothes were verrrry dirty. I wash . . . He eat like horse too," and she laughed.

Waste of time, Contreas thought, but smiled and said, "Glad she took care of you, Rudy. As soon as it's dark I'll take you over west to a friend of mine where you can stay outa sight for a while."

Absorbed in the cards, Timkins merely nodded.

Watson rounded into the packed yard before the office of the Diamond-D, tied his horse to the hitching post and glanced east in time to see the sun lift up over the horizon and thought, Another damn day, and went in and found Alexander just building a fire preparatory to making breakfast.

Glancing at the cot, Watson asked curiously, "How come you don't sleep at the house, Major?"

Alexander placed a full pot of water on the stove and carefully greased a frying pan as he said, "Too many years in the army. Used to sleeping on a cot. Don't like a bed." Breaking eggs in the frying pan and lacing its edges with bacon cut from a side, the mine owner glanced at Watson. "Had breakfast?"

Watson shook his head and suddenly realized he was hungry enough to eat a burro.

Nodding toward a row of cans on a table, the former major said, "Flour over there. How about mixing up a batch of biscuits. They'll cook damn fast in this oven."

Half an hour later as they sat eating wordlessly, the door opened and Ringo slid in, walking like a cat as he crossed the floor. Looking down at the food, he grimaced. "It's barbaric for a man to eat in the morning," he observed.

"You been reading them classics again," Alexander said.

"You should try it, Colonel," Ringo said. "Might learn a thing or two."

"About all a man gets out of that kind of reading is eyestrain and a crick in the neck," Watson said.

Ringo stared at him. "How the hell would you know?"

A small bell of caution went off in Watson's head as he glanced up at the gunfighter and said, "I did some reading years ago, but then I got too involved in making a living."

Ringo smiled. "Just how damn good are you with them guns you wear?" he asked, watching Watson, whose right hand was under the table.

"Well, Johnny, I ain't nearly as fast as you are, but then that's just a freak of nature. Some men are quick, others have to use their heads."

"I never noticed you using either one," Ringo observed dryly.

Looking at Alexander, Watson asked softly, "How bad do you need this pelican?"

"I need both of you, so cut it out," Alexander said irritably, and poured Ringo a cup of coffee.

Still gazing at Watson, Ringo picked up the cup with his

left hand and asked conversationally, "You holding a stingy gun on me under the table?"

Watson grinned. "Yep, and it's aimed right at your gut."

"Mind telling me what caliber it is?"

"Glad to," Watson said. "It's a forty-four."

"Hmmm . . . Too bad. If it was anything lighter, I'd tell you to go ahead and shoot and then I'd blow your butt off before I went down."

"A forty-four's just a little too much to bite on, huh?"

"Just a little bit too much," Ringo agreed, and sipped his coffee, his face expressionless.

Chapter 9

The train rolled slowly along the narrow-gauge track, smoke puffing in quick bursts from its bell-shaped stack, looking for all the world like an angry man punishing his cigar. Ahead lay the small shack that passed for a depot at Fairbanks, an ugly milling town at the head of Walnut Gulch.

Several loungers occupying chairs along the depot platform watched idly as the train approached and wondered why old Canary Jack Fogarty, the engineer, hadn't announced his arrival with the usual half-dozen blasts of the whistle, which invariably frightened any horses that happened to be tied at the hitchrack and sent the station agent's old dog, Bitters, running wildly beneath the platform, where he huddled and peered forth with frightened eyes.

Instead of rolling in with a wail and a blast, the train crept quietly to a stop, gulped smoke from its stack three times and settled down to a steady clamor as one of the passenger cars erupted a dozen hard-looking men with Texas written all over them.

City marshal Boke Bedford had his look, decided they

were none of his business and strolled off down the single
street that was all Fairbanks could lay claim to. As the dust
popped up in little clouds from beneath their boots, the
Texans walked back along the train to a freight car, slid
open a door and pulled forth the heavy loading ramp.

As it struck the ground with a loud clatter, Bedford
glanced around and watched Colonel William Alex step
from a buggy parked in front of the depot and go to meet
the newcomers.

"Now, I wonder what in tarnation that's all about?"
Bedford asked himself.

Back on the platform the bogus colonel strode to where
the men were off-loading their horses and spoke briefly
with a tall man wearing a handlebar mustache.

Neither man paid any attention to the Mexican peon
who sat slouched against the wall of the depot, his hat over
his eyes and in what appeared to be a deep sleep. Behind
the hat, the cool brown eyes of Vent Torrey peered through
the straw webbing of the hat and watched the meeting.

Carefully examining the tall man with the mustache,
Vent was certain he knew him. The Texan was wearing
half boots with a pair of checkered pants tucked into their
tops. His spurs were long-shanked and big-roweled as was
the custom in Texas and the Southwest. Around his hips
he wore a single belt with two guns attached. It was this
rig that rang a bell of recognition in Vent's mind as he
searched himself for a clue as to the man's identity. On the
right hip, the Texan wore a double-action .38, one of the
first made, but it was the second gun rig that had caught
Vent's eye. It was simply a narrow holster with half the
lower end cut away and fastened to the belt in such a
fashion as to put the butt of a single-action Colt .45 square
in line with the man's belt buckle and lying perpendicular
along his belt.

It was a fast-draw rig; all the gunman had to do was jerk

the pistol straight away along the belt line with his right
hand and then spin it out and away so the bore pointed at
the target. The real gimmick was not so much the odd gun
rig. Vent had gone up against his share of such rigs, and
while he continued to breathe, the men who wore them
wound up being buried in them. The trick in the Texan's
outfit was that a man could never be sure which gun he
was going to pull, the one on his hip or the one at his
waist.

Then Vent remembered. The man's name was Pete
Nichols and he had downed his share of men. He was well
known throughout Texas, Kansas and Nebraska as a fast
man with a gun and a man whose gun had a price on it. He
guaranteed results, but the price was high.

Then Vent heard a familiar voice and looked down the
track again. Jim Watson sat his grulla near the freight car,
one leg hooked around the saddle horn, a cigarette dangling from the corner of his mouth. He was wearing the
cougar-skin vest and the gray cavalry hat was pushed to
the back of his head as he talked quietly to Nichols, who
was now mounted on a heavy-shouldered line-back buckskin
with a pronounced jaw and small ears above quick eyes.

So now they're all together and Watson's brought in
some help from his ranch. Vent had heard that Nichols
now worked for Watson as his segundo.

Something caught the two men's attention and they
looked north as Vent glanced that way too. The Fairbanks
marshal was just riding into the mouth of Walnut Gulch,
passing among the mean clutter of miners' shacks that
clung to the sides of the rocky slopes.

Looking back at Nichols and Watson, Vent saw the
rancher nod and watched Nichols ride to where a short,
powerfully built man with a huge gut hanging over his belt
sat a big bay horse and speak briefly to him, then watched
as the man followed the marshal up the gulch.

Thinking about it, Vent decided to see what Watson had in mind. Rising slowly to his feet, the Missourian, mimicking the abject shuffle of a Mexican peon, wandered off the platform and moved casually in among the mean shacks east of the depot. As he walked along, he did not look back but instead watched the faces of the men he passed, noting they first looked at him, then at the men in front of the depot.

Probably watching me, he thought, but steeled himself to keep walking. A hundred yards from the station, a narrow cut in a low ridge ran away from the collection of shacks at an oblique angle, and Vent, taking his time, moved into and around a bend, then stopped and walked back, removed the sombrero and carefully looked along the trail. One of Watson's men was following him, on a little black horse he was having trouble handling. It kept trying to turn back and the rider kept jerking the reins.

Herd bound, Vent thought and looking around, saw a large boulder ten feet above the canyon floor and quickly climbed behind it and settled down to wait. First he heard the sound of a horse's hooves, then a man cursed, and horse and rider rounded the bend and came on as Vent watched. When the man was directly beneath his hiding place, Vent drew his gun from beneath the serape he wore, eared the hammer back and said softly, "Hello, amigo. Looking for me?"

The man jerked the horse up and turned his head to stare at Vent, then said, "Pete was right. You're just too damn tall to be a Mexican peon. And hell, man, you don't even walk like a Mex."

"So what you aim to do about it?" Vent asked, pushing the hat to the back of his head and settling himself against the rock.

"Damned if I know." The rider shrugged. "It's your play. You got the pistola."

"Reckon maybe I'll just plug you," Vent said conversationally.

The man stared at him. "Why?"

"Don't like the way you wear your hat." Vent grinned.

Not sure whether Vent meant it or not, the man let his hand move closer to his hip. The move drew no response from Vent, who merely kept looking at the man.

"You'd like me to make a try, now wouldn't you?"

"Well, compadre, it might just salve my conscience a little, seeing as how I've already plugged four or five gents who were unarmed. Might make me feel better, although I reckon by now I'm beyond redemption."

"You fire off that pistol and you're gonna be knee deep in Texans," the rider warned.

"Now just how the hell's that gonna help you?" Vent asked, using the barrel of his pistol to push his hat back farther.

The move was not missed by the rider, but he still refused to be baited. Instead he moved his hand farther away from the ,45 he wore and waited, his eyes showing nothing.

"What's your handle, hombre?" Vent asked.

"What the hell's that to you?"

"Just like to know who I'm about to kill," Vent told him, and leveled the .44 on the rider's stomach.

"Name's Bates . . . Carl Bates," the rider finally said sullenly.

"Defang yourself, Mr. Bates, and do it now," Vent suddenly ordered, and watched with satisfaction as the Texan carefully lifted his gun free and dropped it into the dust with the remark, "Hell of a way to treat a good gun."

"Shouldn't make no difference to a dead man," Vent said reasonably.

Clambering down the bank, Vent picked up the gun, then walked to the left side of the horse. "Foot outa the stirrup.'' When Bates complied, he mounted behind him and said, "On down the draw," and placed the barrel of the pistol against the rider's spine.

Around the next bend they came to where the Appaloosa stood ground-tied, and dropping off, Vent went to the big horse and stepped lightly into leather. "See you around, pard. Thanks for the horseback ride," and rode off without looking back.

He was fifty feet from Bates when the man suddenly gigged his horse into a run and whirled him back toward the station. Halfway through the turn, the saddle latigo suddenly gave way, hurling Bates against the side of the bank and dropping the rig beneath the horse's belly.

Watching the horse run wildly toward the bend as it kicked Bates's saddle to pieces, Vent shrugged, put away his knife and observed, "Appaloosa, that's the trouble with them double rigs. If the front cinch goes, the saddle slides under the horse's belly still hooked to the back rig and there goes one good saddle," and not looking back, he rode on around another bend and then put the Appy to a hard run, quartering toward the upper end of Walnut Gulch.

He broke out above the gulch where it cut through the Contention City–Tombstone stage road. Sitting his horse among a stand of stunted saguaros, he watched Boke Bedford ride along the floor of the gulch below him. Looking to Bedford's rear, he saw the heavy-set rider Nichols had sent after the marshal and now the man had his rifle unlimbered and was holding it across the pommel of his saddle.

Riding down a side gulch, Vent suddenly broke out in front of the fat man on the big bay and, sliding the Appaloosa to a halt, sat staring at him. The fat man had pulled in his horse and was starting to lift the rifle barrel.

"Do that and I'll kill you," Vent said.

"Get ta hell outa my way, Mex," the Texan snarled, and continued swinging the rifle in line.

"To hell with it," Vent said, and drew the .44 and fired one shot. The bullet caught the fat man at the bridge of the nose and blew the top of his head off, lifting the man a foot out of the leather on impact. Dropping back into the saddle again, the body hung there as the horse began to sidestep, then ponderously fell into the dirt.

Riding off to one side of the gulch, Vent holstered his gun and waited. In less than a minute, he heard horses' hooves, then Bedford rounded the bend at a driving run and upon seeing the sprawled body in the middle of the trail, slammed back on the reins and skidded to a stop.

Only then did he see Vent, and cursing, his hand dived for his gun.

Vent's gun flashed up in a sudden arc, catching the marshal's hand a good six inches from his. "Nice try," Vent said.

"Who the hell are you?" Bedford asked.

"Me, oh I'm just the feller that dropped that bushwhacker that's been trailing you ever since you rode outa Fairbanks."

Bedford scratched the back of his neck, looking quizzically at first the body, then Vent. "Who's the stiff?"

"Feller works for Colonel Alex. Alex sent him after you."

Staring at Vent's sombrero and serape, Bedford asked his own question. "What's a white man doing dressed like a Mex?"

"I like chili and beans." Vent grinned and, holstering his pistol, began rolling a cigarette.

"You look familiar," Bedford said accusingly.

"Name's Vent Torrey." He licked the cigarette closed, tucked it in the corner of his mouth, and fired it up. Blowing a trail of smoke, Vent watched the marshal.

"Vent Torrey . . . the feller they call Leatherhand?"

"Go to the head of the class, Marshal," Vent said.

"Well, I'll be damned!"

"Maybe," Vent observed, then asked again: "Where was you heading?"

"Why, I was gonna go see Wyatt Earp and let him know a bunch of Texas waddies had hit the county. . . ."

"Friend of Earp's, are you?"

"Reckon."

"See ya." Vent turned the Appy and started to ride away when Bedford suddenly called, "Hey, Mr. Torrey, thanks for takin' that feller off my trail. Hell, he coulda plugged me."

"No charge," Vent said, and rode around a bend.

As soon as he was clear of the marshal, he put the Appaloosa to a hard run and half an hour later pulled the blowing animal in under a stand of paloverde just east of the Tombstone boothill, where he found the Preacher boiling coffee and cooking bacon over a smokeless fire. Stepping down, Vent led the horse around for several minutes, then loosened the cinch, removed the bridle and turned it out to feed.

Watching him wordlessly, the Preacher finally observed, "Someday, boy, you're gonna do that and that old pony's just naturally gonna up and split the wind right when you need him most."

"Don't reckon he'll do that, Preacher. Old feller's Injun-trained. He'll stand until hell claims him."

Walking to the fire, he picked up a tin cup, forked several pieces of bacon onto a plate and watched as the Preacher raked a blackened bundle of leaves from the coals and opened them to reveal a dozen well-cooked biscuits. Using the hot bread as sandwich material, the two men sat comfortably by the fire and ate their meager meal, drank away the pot until only the grounds were left and then Vent rolled a cigarette and the Preacher dug out a cigar.

"See anything at Fairbanks?" he asked.

"Yep, it was just as we overheard at the mine. Watson's brought in a bunch of Texas lead throwers, probably off his ranch."

Grinning bleakly, the Preacher said, "I guess it was worth the risk, us creeping up on old Alex's office and eavesdropping that way."

Vent smiled as he recalled raising his head to the window and discovering himself looking straight at Johnny Ringo with a roomful of gun-toting miners. Thinking about it now, he looked at the Preacher and asked, "You reckon he'll get those miners to side him?"

"Hard telling." The Preacher shook his head. "I'm more worried about those Texans of Jim's."

"Ever hear of a gent named Pete Nichols?" Vent asked.

The Preacher looked up sharply. "Hell, yes. Pistol fighter. Laid a few good men in the ground. A damn tough man to boot. He's no flash gunman."

"So I hear," Vent said, and thought, now they got Ringo, Contreas, Watson and Nichols . . . and wondered why the hell he and the Preacher didn't just ride away. "Any reason to stay in this game?"

Looking into the flames, the Preacher thought a minute, then said, "None. If I followed my instincts, I'd just ride out, but they's that money Birch stole. It's got to be at the mine and me, I guess I could use the reward about now. How about you?"

Vent grinned. "I ain't flush by any means. Course I can always head for Colorado and pick up my share of the returns from the Lost Lake Ranch. Sis, she keeps it for me until I need it."

Thinking about that, the Preacher said softly, "I reckon it's a good thing for a feller to have somebody who worries about him. Me, I've kinda outlived everybody who cared . . .'ceptin' this damn Watson pup and now he turns sour.''

Vent nodded once. "I guess you just put the name on why we should hang around. It ain't the money and it ain't a matter of pride. It's a matter of stomping a snake who rode flank to flank with us, used us and now is whip-sawing us.''

The Preacher stood up and looked west toward the Diamond-D mine. "I guess I'm gonna have to kill that damn whelp.''

"You want me to stomp that snake?"

"No, it's my job.''

"Don't seem right, a man forced to gun his own kin. . . .''

"We'll see," the Preacher said softly, and went to see to his horse as Vent rose and began tossing the cooking utensils into a saddlebag.

Tombstone was no quieter than usual when Vent and the Preacher walked their horses along Fremont Street. Over on Allen, the sudden blare of a rinky-dink piano split the night as somebody pushed a saloon door wide, then it faded to a dull thunder with the closing of the door. Shouts and curses funneled along Fifth Street as they moved south, only to be replaced by more of the same at Fourth. A sudden roar of shots heralded some drunken cowboy telling the world he was in town and wild and woolly and full of fleas and never curried below the knees. His slugs blasted a street lamp into sudden darkness on the corner of Allen and Fourth. At the first shot, Vent had looked that way and saw the narrow streaks of fire leap from the man's gun and smash the light. He was standing spraddle-legged in the middle of the intersection with gun still upraised when somebody opened a door behind him and lamplight outlined his form briefly. In that moment, Vent saw the tall shape of Wyatt Earp materialize out of the night, an arm rise and fall and the cowboy pitch into the dust.

Pulling in sharply, Vent said, "Let's drift over near city hall. I figure Earp will be along shortly with a prisoner."

Riding on, they swung in beneath the building's overhanging side roof and waited in deep shadow. Five minutes passed and then Earp appeared around the corner of Fourth, leading a dazed and bleeding prisoner. As he passed their hiding place, some inner instinct warned him he wasn't alone, and suddenly tensing, his hand dropped to his gun, but he kept walking, stepping to the outside of the cowboy and using him as a shield.

"Howdy, Marshal," Vent said softly.

Earp stopped and half turned, and then Vent could see the bared gun in his fist and said, "No need for that."

"So it's you," Earp said, and holstered the gun. "Stay put until I salt this feller down for the night, then I'll be along."

When he came out of the building, Earp did not directly approach them, but instead stopped opposite their hiding place and under the cover of lighting a cigar, said quietly, "Go on down street. Watch for a dobe with a flowerpot hanging beside the door. That's Doc's place. You'll find Kate and Miss Brown there. I'll be along directly," and he dropped the spent match and moved on.

Vent and the Preacher remained where they were for a long five minutes, carefully watching the street, then when nothing showed, left the building and rode south past the OK Corral, passing beneath the light hanging over its gate, then on into shadows.

"One of you boys got a light?" a voice suddenly asked, and Vent and the Preacher both drew their pistols and aligned them on the dark shadow that detached itself from a building. The faint light from the OK Corral revealed a tall, thin man wearing glasses who held nothing more deadly in his hand than a long thin cigar.

Glancing at the guns, the man said, "You boys seem a little jumpy tonight."

"Kinda risky, coming at a man out of the dark that way," the Preacher observed.

"Sorry. Name's Fly, C. S. Fly. Run a boarding house here on Fremont. Also operate a photography studio."

Vent leaned down and fired his cigarette, making sure the match did not illuminate his face. As the quick flash of the match shot prisms of fire from the man's glasses, he said, "Much obliged, gents. If you ever need a picture taken, drop around. Got the best props in the business," and he moved on down Fremont, his tall stooped figure slowly fading from view.

When they found Kate's place, Vent left the Preacher with the horses and knocked on the door.

"Who's there?" a woman's voice inquired. There was no fear in it, only a question.

"Vent Torrey," he said softly, and waited.

When the door opened, it wasn't a woman who greeted them, but Doc Holliday himself. He stood just beyond the light, gun in hand, and asked mildly, "You're out kinda late, ain't ya, Mr. Torrey?"

Chuckling, Vent said, "The Preacher's out there with the horses. Got a place we can put them outa sight?"

"Round back. I'll meet you there," and the door closed softly.

Vent went and picked up the Appaloosa's reins and, followed by the Preacher, walked down a narrow alley to where a corral held three horses. Opening the gate, Vent let the Preacher pass, then followed him inside and with Holliday's help quickly off-saddled and fed the mounts.

When they entered the house from the back door, they

found Angel Brown standing before a fireplace talking to a robust woman with large breasts, a full figure and bright, intelligent eyes.

Nodding at her, Holliday said, "This is Kate Elder. You know Miss Brown."

Vent smiled at Angel and she stared at him as if she were seeing a ghost. "I thought . . . we thought . . . you were dead," she said hesitantly.

"Bad report." Vent grinned.

"They tried," the Preacher said dryly.

Vent and the Preacher remained at Kate Elder's for two days, then Bat Masterson stopped by with Holliday and solemnly shook hands with the two men. "I'm on my way to Denver," he said. "Big game there."

The Preacher smiled and glanced at Vent. "If it lasts long enough, I'll join you in a couple of weeks."

Nodding, Masterson said, "Tamp her light, boys," and went away, leaving Holliday to explain to Kate where he had been for two days.

His answer was simple. "Been in a poker game at the Oriental."

"You win?" Kate asked.

"Yep," Holliday answered, and went in search of the whiskey. When he returned, Wyatt Earp was there. Looking at the marshal, Holliday asked, "You find out what's going on?"

Earp turned to Vent. "Feller you saved from a bullet in the back said to tell you he owes you a drink."

"If he don't start watching his back trail, he ain't gonna live long enough to set it up," Vent observed dryly.

"He told me something else," Earp said. "Seems as how them Texans has joined up with Colonel Alex's boys from the mine and they're all headed for Gleeson."

"What the hell's at Gleeson?" the Preacher asked.

"Old mining town. About used up," Holliday said.

"Behan a part of this?" Vent inquired.

"He's playing a cold deck," Earp said. "Staying to hell out."

"I thought he was on his way to drag the colonel back here by his spurs," the Preacher observed.

Holliday grinned. "Too busy trying to figure out where you boys went. Couldn't be bothered with the colonel."

The Preacher accepted a drink from Holliday and lowered his lanky frame into a chair. "Reckon you boys got a right to know what's going on out there at the Diamond-D. Jim Watson was at the Bandera Hills Massacre, but somehow he survived. He come to me down in west Texas and wanted my help to run the murderers to ground."

Looking at Earp, Vent said softly, "Only two left alive, besides the man you know as Colonel Alex. Timkins is one of them. The other is Anselamo Contreas."

Holliday and Earp looked at each other, then Earp cleared his throat. "Well, I'll be double-damned."

"Colonel Alex is really Major William J. Alexander, former Confederate officer at Fort Verde, Texas, and a graduate of West Point. He's the man who stood by and allowed his troopers to hang the Bandera innocents."

Earp's eyes were bleak as he heard the Preacher out, then he turned to Holliday and pointed out, "These boys are heading into a stacked deck if they ride to Gleeson. The marshal there sits in Alex's hip pocket and pays revenue to Johnny Behan. Hell, Ike and Billy Clanton spend half their time in that place gambling when they ain't south of the border rustling Mex cattle." He thought about it for a moment, then said, "Maybe so we should trail along . ''

Holliday shook his head. "You got too much at stake here, Wyatt. Me, I can get into a ruckus like this one and nobody will even mention it, unless Behan finds some way to turn it against me.''

''Damn, but I hate to stand down, Doc. You boys are up against some of the best. Ringo's no fading rose and Pete Nichols is sudden swift with a handgun.''

Looking at Vent, Holliday said mildly, ''We ain't exactly lilies of the valley, Wyatt.''

''No, you ain't, but that's still a heap of guns to go up against,'' Wyatt argued. ''They's Watson, and according to that telegram I sent, he never was in Fredericksburg. What I didn't mention is he's already laid seven men in the ground, including Al Avery.''

The Preacher and Holliday looked at each other. ''Avery, huh,'' the Preacher said. ''I saw him in a standup fight in Tascosas few years back. He was hell on little red wheels and quicker than a snapping tug chain.''

''If Contreas and Timkins join up with them, it'll take a damn army to winkle 'em out,'' Earp observed.

Vent thought about it for a long minute, then slowly began to smile. ''And just maybe I know where to find that army. Let's ride for Dragoon.''

Angel came from the other side of the room then and touched Vent's sleeve. ''I won't try to talk you out of this, Vent Torrey, but dammit, you be careful. Enough good men have gone down in this thing.''

''Hell, they ain't molded a bullet that'll kill that feller,'' the Preacher said, and grinned his wolf's grin.

Holliday glanced at Wyatt. ''Be seeing you, compadre. Keep my seat warm at the Oriental,'' and led the way out back, where they saddled the horses and rode quietly north.

Two hours later, Vent led the little group of riders into a dark canyon and pulled in before a mean shack. A horse was tied to the crude hitching post in front of the place. Vent checked the brand and found he didn't know it, then knocked on the door.

"Get the hell away from here," somebody called from inside.

Grinning, Vent calmly opened the door and strolled in, finding Noona and a cowboy who still wore his hat sitting up in bed staring at him.

"Who the hell are you?" the cowboy demanded, reaching for his gun where it dangled in its holster from a bedpost.

"The man that'll kill you if you touch that gun," Vent said mildly, then nodded at Noona, who was smiling gleefully. "Lady, how you be?"

Staring at her, the cowboy demanded, "Who is this waddy? What the hell's he doing coming in here like this?"

Vent picked up the man's pants and tossed them to him. "Get dressed . . . Now."

Noona patted him on the cheek. "It's all right, cowboy. You come back tomorrow and Mama will give you a reride."

The cowboy slid out of bed and began fumbling on his pants, grumbling to himself as Vent and the Indian woman watched. When he was finally dressed, he glanced at his gun. "Mind if I take that along? This here country ain't too safe a place for a defanged man to be riding around in."

"Go ahead, take it." Vent nodded toward the door. "They's a couple other boys outside. They're a damn sight meaner than I am, so walk kinda careful when you leave." When the cowboy had ridden away, Vent looked at Noona and asked, "How soon can you put me in touch with Deerslayer?"

"About two minutes." She smiled. "He's asleep in the cave."

"Will you bring him down here, please?"

Touching his side, she asked, "How's the hurt?"

"Fine, thanks to you," he said, and watched her leave.

When she returned, she was followed by the tall powerful frame of Deerslayer, who solemnly shook hands with Vent, then went and squatted against the wall. "My friend, what brings you here?"

"I need help," Vent said simply.

"Name it."

"How many men can you get on short notice?"

Unhesitatingly, Deerslayer said, "Twenty, with rifles."

"Will they fight with me?"

"They will go where I tell them to go." The Indian touched his chest lightly with four fingers. "I am the kinsman of the great Vitorio. They will obey me."

"I am in a war with the man who operates the Diamond-D mine. He has thirty men. I have the two you see outside."

Noona smiled. "The one called Holliday is well known among the Apaches. He is a great warrior. The old one is also a great warrior, for it shows in his face, as it lies in yours also, Leatherhand."

Vent lifted the leather-clad gunhand and gazed at it for a long moment, then said simply, "It is not enough. It needs a left hand to help it."

Deerslayer walked to the door. "Where do we meet?"

"Our enemy has ridden to the town of Gleeson," Vent said.

Nodding, Deerslayer pointed toward Tombstone and in a cold deadly voice, said, "Watch the line of the sky in that direction after the moon starts its downward swing tonight, and when you see the red flames leap to play with the night ghosts above the Diamond-D, you ride to meet me at the Tombstone stage road."

Vent nodded and watched Deerslayer slip through the door. He did not hear his horse when it left.

Turning then to Noona, he took her by the shoulders and kissed her soundly. "If my heart was not promised to one who lives in the other world, I would take you away with me tonight."

Looking straight into his eyes, she observed, "The dead stay dead unless the night breezes call them, but even when that happens they are cold and of no use to a man whose blood runs hot in his veins. Take what you find and forget the dead one. She will not care, for she has put aside the things of this world."

"I made a promise. A warrior does not break a promise." Vent walked to the door, and as he passed out into the yard, a quick picture of Lilly running across the street in Crested Butte as the bullets of the Hawkses cut her down tore at him and his eyes filled with blood and hate roared in his temples while Holliday and the Preacher, catching a glimpse of his features as he passed through the light from a window, were silent, only following his brooding figure.

Holliday had seen his share of berserkers and the Preacher recognized the swelling drive of blood lust when he saw it and marveled, for it was the first time he had ever seen Vent Torrey in savage anger.

Far to the south, Anselamo Contreas rode along beside Rudy Timkins and listened to the little gunman's inane chattering about what he planned to do once he had his cut of the Alexander operation and was safely away in Mexico.

"Me, I'm gonna get me a big jug of vino, a Mex gal wearing one of them long, swishy dresses with the top half cut so low a man can look clean to her belly button and a big bowl of tortillas and beans, and pay the band to cut loose with 'Cinco de Mayo' and whoop her up."

Contreas smiled grimly in the dark as they passed through a dark canyon, thinking, Little man, the only place you are going tonight is to hell and I hope the red-faced one has the flames poked high.

When they cleared the canyon, Timkins suddenly pulled in his horse and cursed. "Feels like this old bronc done picked up a rock," and he slid off and lifted a hoof as Contreas rode a little past him and stopped to wait impatiently. When Timkins' bullet hit Contreas in the back, he only had time to realize he had been outsmarted by the outlaw as he toppled from the saddle, a great sadness descending on him as the blackness claimed him and he heard Timkins chuckle and mutter softly, "So you figured I didn't know what you was up to, huh, Mex? Well, I saw you make that throat-cutting move to your greaser gal in the mirror. I knowed what you planned," and then Contreas died as Timkins began pulling off his fancy black boots.

Chapter 10

The huddle of buildings that was Gleeson sat dark and brooding on their hill overlooking a barren sweep of plateau where nothing grew but stunted saguaros and a bushy paloverde, whose mass of yellow blossoms caught the fitful rays of a full moon and huddled in the night like some ghostly specter.

An owl's solemn call was suddenly interrupted by the clatter of hard-driven hooves, then a long, lean line of riders passed in front of the paloverde and slanted through the entrance gate to the town, rousing a dog from its sleep beneath the porch of a mercantile store half a block down the unnamed main street.

The riders were silent as they pulled their horses to a stop in front of a false-fronted building with a black sign that said "saloon." They trooped inside and lined up at the bar in the fitful light from a set of gas lamps that hung from the rafters on each end of a long room. As the men waited for their bottles, they glanced around and the light flashed from eyes that were wary and hands that hung close to guns.

The tall, dignified figure of Colonel Alex held stage center as he looked at Tub Baldwin, the three-hundred-pound owner of the place, and ordered drinks for all.

One of the men, the cold-eyed Pete Nichols, tolled a man off and sent him to sit on the front steps with glass in hand and a second man to cover the rear with a Winchester.

Jim Watson leaned against the plank and stared into the amber fluid in his glass, then glanced at Baldwin. "What kinda poison is this?"

Baldwin was no fool; neither had he survived on the frontier for thirty years by being reckless. Right now he could recognize a war party when he saw one and he wanted no part of them. He knew it was the Ringo Kid who stood at his bar and slowly turned a shot glass full of whiskey in tight circles on the wood and looked at nothing.

"It's a brand I get for two dollars a barrel from an Indian whiskey drummer who comes through here from up in the Dragoons," Baldwin said with a straight face.

Alex smiled dryly and the Ringo Kid looked up and nodded as if to compliment the tubby bartender on his sense of humor.

Watson tossed off the whiskey. "They oughta hang that damned Injun. Gimme another. . . ."

Alex picked up his bottle and walked to a table near the back of the room. "Wonder where the hell that damn Mex is?" he said to Ringo.

"Probably laid up with that señorita of his," Ringo said.

"Hell, it ain't like him not to show. All he had to do was put that snake Timkins down and come on here. No big chore."

Watson had come over and now he said softly, "Maybe he underestimated Timkins. Hell, that little gunnie managed to break outa the Prescott jail and outride a posse all the way to Kingman, then get down here without Bratton nailing him, and Bratton was no amateur.''

"He died like one," Ringo observed.

"Any man can go down if he's ambushed in the dark," Ringo said, then grinned and looked straight at Watson. "I notice you boys didn't bring in Leatherhand's scalp.''

Pete Nichols had walked up, drained his glass, refilled it from Alex's bottle and asked, "That feller Leatherhand, he as fast as they say?''

"I wouldn't know," Ringo said. "I never tried him.''

"Them that has are all riding the wind," Watson said.

"You see him in a fandango, did ya?" Ringo asked.

Watson nodded. "He's faster than anything I ever saw. They ain't a man alive can beat him, and I'd bet big money on that.''

"What about Hickok . . . or Holliday, for that matter?'' Nichols asked.

"I believe Torrey could beat them both," Watson told him.

Alex shrugged. "So, we plant a bullet in his back. No muss and no fuss. He's just dead, that's all; just dead.''

Ringo stared at him, then slowly began to smile. "A lot of men have tried that game and none have ever brought it off. Colonel, you know how many men Leatherhand has put down?''

"No, and I care less." Alex lifted his glass and drained it.

"Well, I'll tell you. They say he's notched his gun on maybe thirty or thirty five. Maybe more than that.''

Alex shrugged. "Bill Longley took down thirty six and he still wound up doing the hemp fandango.''

The Texan who had been guarding the front of the saloon came in and walked back to the colonel's table. "Big glow off toward your mine, Colonel. Looks like one hell of a fire.''

Alex sat very still, then said softly, "So. I should have guessed that. My fault."

Watson stared at him. "You ain't got much when the mine goes, Colonel."

"It'll rebuild," Alex said, and returned to his whiskey.

A Watson man rose and went to the door. "Riders coming, Jim."

Watson walked to the door and stood to one side of it, hand on his gun, as the rest of his men fanned out into dark corners and waited, their eyes flickering firefly gleams in the dim hall.

Watson turned and said, "Your men, Colonel," and moved back down the room as several tough-looking miners came through the door and stood in a line in front of the colonel.

Looking them over, Alex said quietly, "I'm paying you boys fighting wages tonight. From here we ride to Tombstone, and when we leave, that bastard wearing the leather glove on his right hand will be boot-hill bait, and so will Doc Holliday and Wyatt Earp if they interfere."

No one said anything. Alex rose and walked to the door and stood looking out into the moonlit street, then stepped outside onto the sidewalk, drink in hand, and paused there, the light from the door casting an eerie glow across his face.

"Big mistake, Major Alexander," Vent said softly from across the street. He stood on the sidewalk in front of an assay office.

Alex's arm stopped halfway to his face as he stared at the tall lean shadow, then Vent said just as softly, "Draw your gun, Major Alexander," and Alexander, knowing he was dead and suddenly not caring, made his try and Vent shot him through the chest and watched the heavy .44 slug kick him backward through the batwings and into the saloon, where he landed flat on his back in the sawdust of the floor. He stared upward at the swinging lamp and said distinctly, "That's the last one. They're all dead," and his arm dropped and he was still.

"Damn," one of the miners suddenly swore, and then the place erupted gunmen into the street as Vent crouched over his smoking .44 and pounded shots into their midst, tearing dying screams from wide-stretched mouths.

Suddenly Doc Holliday appeared three buildings down from where Vent stood and, crouching over his blazing .45s, shot a man loose from the porch support he was using as cover and another backward into the saloon, where he landed in a pile of glass from the window the big slug had kicked him into.

A high Rebel yell tore the night as the Preacher, guns blazing, came striding along the dusty way, firing first his right hand gun and then his left.

The men in front of the saloon vanished up alleys and into narrow slots between buildings as the residents of the town began shouting for the marshal.

Half of Watson's men ducked out the back door with Watson leading them and ran straight into a murderous wall of lead from the heavy Sharps rifles carried by Deerslayer's Apaches. Men screamed and fell and rose and ran aimlessly into the desert, only to be run down by hard-riding Indians and cut down with tomahawks.

Watson, having survived the first charge, ducked down an alley and found himself corkscrewed between Deerslayer's Apaches and Vent's gunfighter crew.

Leaning against the building, he carefully aimed and fired and watched an Apache driven backward from his horse, and fired again and scored another hit, then they had his position and he ran back toward the main street as half a dozen slugs ripped splinters from the corner of the building and someone inside screamed high and wild.

As Vent crouched over his gun and punched out the

empties and reloaded, he could hear a baby crying somewhere, then he saw Watson break from an alley and leg it south toward the tall gate leading into the main street. He was twenty feet from the twin posts when the Preacher suddenly appeared. Watson stopped and stood facing the old man, his gun bared in his hand, and Vent heard him say, "I had to do it, I had no choice."

The Preacher merely looked at Watson, and then the rancher shook his head and, ignoring the sporadic firing behind him, said, "I sold those men out at Bandera. They were carrying ten thousand dollars and they hid it. I knew where and I traded my life for the money."

There was pleading in Watson's voice now and all the old banter was gone as he looked helplessly at the Preacher and laughed dully. "Hell, Alexander and his men would have hung me too. I gave them the money for my life."

Then the Preacher spoke and there was a lull in the firing as he asked, "Alexander was blackmailing you? Was that it?"

"Yes, damn him. He wanted enough money to get his mine out of hock. He was mortgaged to the trigger guard."

"Why didn't you just kill him?" the Preacher asked, and there was real curiosity in his voice.

"I decided to break him and take his mine instead." Watson shrugged.

"Bad decision," the Preacher said bleakly, and lifted his gun and fired, and the shock of the bullet spun Watson around facing Vent. As he stood there with blood squirting into the dust from the hole in his chest and looked at the Missourian wonderingly, he said, "So this is the way it feels," then his face caved in and he fell and lay still.

The Preacher strode up the street, and when he passed the body, he did not look down.

"Leatherhand!" someone shouted from near the saloon,

and Vent turned and Pete Nichols was standing there with his guns holstered, waiting.

Vent dropped his .44 into leather and turned and walked to within twenty five feet of the Texan. "I could let you ride out," and then saw by Nichols' face it would never do and let a cold smile flicker and touch his eyes. "There's always a stopping place. You call the cards."

Nichols said, "Reckon now's as good as any other time," and went for his gun. Vent had been watching the right hand, and when it streaked for the gun at Nichols' waist, the Missourian drew so fast the Texan's hand was still three inches away when Vent's bullet tore through his body, kicking him sideways.

Nichols slowly righted himself and, shaking his head, said, "Damn, this here's sure a night for dying," and fell into the street, rolled over and died with his eyes still open.

Vent punched out the empties from his .44 and then Holliday came from north of town and stopped to look at the dead Nichols. "The great leveler, old man death," and came on to meet the Preacher and Vent in the center of the dusty thoroughfare.

"I lost that bastard, Ringo," Holliday said. "He gave me the slip at the edge of town."

Vent looked up then and Deerslayer rode between the buildings and stopped in front of Vent, nodding solemnly. "They have all gone across the river to ride no more. I have lost two brave men to the guns of the man Watson."

Pointing to Watson's body, Vent said, "He lies there. The old one has killed him. He was kin to the old one. It was his right to take his life."

Deerslayer looked at the Preacher. "It is hard to send off a kinsman. My heart is heavy for you, my friend."

The Preacher reached a bony hand to Deerslayer and shook the Apache's hand, and then Deerslayer turned and rode a short distance along the street, looked back, grinned widely, gave forth a wild Apache shriek and galloped through the town gate. As he broke free into the desert, a long line of headbanded shadows rode in behind him and he led them toward the Dragoons.

A stocky man wearing bib overalls and a calico shirt came shuffling along the street, and as he stopped in front of Holliday, the gleam of a badge tossed back the light from the saloon lamps. "I'm the marshal here, sir, what's going on?"

Holliday sighed. "Go away, little man, or damned if I don't punch your ticket this night."

When the marshal started to bluster, Vent took his arm and led him down the street and turned him loose with the soft admonishment, "Go, Mr. Marshal, and sin no more."

They had one drink in Tub Baldwin's saloon to celebrate their victory, then satiated, they rode out the high gate and left the town of Gleeson to bury the dead.

Epilogue

The nights had cooled off in the desert and soft winds carrying a promise of winter were teasing the paloverde as Vent and the Preacher stopped at the stage station on Allen Street where Angel Brown, a satchel containing $50,000 in her hand, was just boarding. Seeing them, she turned and came to Vent's stirrup. "Mr. Torrey, you remember what I told you when you were in Kelly?"

"Yes ma'am," Vent said.

"The offer still stands." She smiled as if she owned a great secret and boarded the stage just as a troop of smartly dressed cavalry trotted into town from the north and pulled up before the stage station.

Sitting astride a tall bay horse was Colonel Royce C. Bedlam, and Vent grinned as the colonel glanced at him, then turned his horse smartly, said something to a young lieutenant and rode to where Vent sat the Appaloosa.

Saluting, he said, "Mr. Torrey, it appears you and I always seem to be crossing trails. I hope things have gone well with you."

Vent nodded. "They have, Colonel. They have."

"We are in your debt for the Major Alexander thing," he said. "We have been looking for that man for a long time."

"My pleasure," Vent said, and the colonel again saluted and rode back, spoke briefly to Angel Brown through the stage window and then led the coach north along Allen Street.

As its dust faded away, Vent and the Preacher rode to the Oriental and found Holliday and Wyatt Earp standing on the sidewalk enjoying their first cigar of the day.

Vent stared at them disapprovingly. "You'd think the town marshal would do something about these here ne'er-do-wells hanging about the streets of Tombstone, now wouldn't you?"

The Preacher grinned frostily.

Holliday let a light touch his eyes briefly, then sobering, said, "They found Contreas. He was out in the desert. Somebody plugged him in the back and stripped off his fancy rig-out and left him in his long-handles."

Vent nodded. "Reckon old Timkins is riding a mighty fancy saddle these days."

"Looks like you boys are all packed and ready to leave," Earp said.

"Gone over the hill to see what's on the other side," Vent told them.

"And you, Preacher?" Holliday asked.

"Off to Denver to see if Masterson's still got that game going."

Earp nodded, then turned to Holliday. "Got word. The Clantons are coming into the OK Corral tonight to have a powwow."

Vent looked at the Preacher and then asked Earp, "You fellers need any help? We could stick around."

Earp shook his head. "We'll take care of it. Them boys is all bluff."

Nodding, Vent turned his horse, and he and the Preacher rode north along Allen Street.

It was October 26, 1881.

George G. Gilman

ADAM STEELE

More bestselling western adventure from Pinnacle, America's #1 series publisher!

☐	40378-X Death Trail #12	$1.50
☐	41452-8 Tarnished Star #19	$1.75
☐	41453-6 Wanted for Murder #20	$1.95
☐	41454-4 Wagons East #21	$1.95
☐	41455-2 Big Game #22	$1.95
☐	41914-7 Fort Despair #23	$1.95
☐	41916-3 Steele's War: The Woman #25	$2.25
☐	41917-1 Steele's War: The Preacher #26	$2.50